DEAD MAN'S

FUGUE

CASEY NEUMILLER

First printing, 2013

ISBN-13: 978-0615879321 (Shamrock Concepts)
ISBN-10: 0615879322

Shamrock Concepts
1310 4th Ave
Washburn, ND 58577

To the Angry Villagers:
Thank you for always providing motivation to write, in the
form of torches and pitchforks.

I

THE MAN STARTLED AWAKE, THRASHING about as he tried to get his bearings. Or rather, he *would* have started thrashing around, had his arms and legs not been firmly bound.

The world around him was tinted red. He blinked, trying to clear the haze from his vision, before realizing that he was submerged in fluid. The man almost panicked then, but oxygen continued to flow steadily through the mask strapped over his nose and mouth and allowed him to remain calm.

Where am I? What's going on?

He tried to think, to analyze the situation, but his brain seemed to be fogged over. He squinted and tried to peer through the liquid. *I'm in a tank. Oh.*

I'm in a tank.

He glanced up and saw the level of fluid already beginning to drop. His thoughts were still crawling along at a torpid pace, but the sights around him were beginning to coalesce into a picture he recognized.

Oh, shit. I'm in a cloning *tank. If I'm here, that means my life insurance policy was invoked, which means I'm dead somewhere.*

As the sticky fluid dropped past eye level, he saw a man in a med coat standing outside the tank. The doctor raised his eyebrows in an unspoken question. The man in the tank nodded in understanding. *Yes, I'm under control.* A moment later the restraints around his arms and legs snapped open, allowing him to begin moving. He reached up with unsteady hands and pulled the mask from his face, then let it dangle from the connecting tube running out of the cloning cylinder.

Mind is fuzzy because of the mind-flash, he thought. *I'm...who am I? Rake. That's my name. Rake Weston.*

The fluid finished draining out the bottom of the tube with a gurgle. He rolled his shoulders experimentally, feeling strength start to flow into his muscles. The tube itself began to shake, and a moment later it was lifted away into the ceiling, leaving him standing - well, leaning - against the platform where he had been strapped.

The man in the white lab coat approached him with an outstretched hand. "Mr. Weston, I'm Doctor Valance."

"How long?" Rake asked hoarsely.

"It's been two weeks since you last re-flashed your memory," the doctor said, requiring no further clarification. "We received the end-of-life signal this morning and began the wake-up process. We'll need to run you through the mental and physical tests to ensure the memory flash is holding. After all," Doctor Valance added with a smile, "I'm sure you wouldn't be happy if your insurance policy wasn't fulfilled to the letter of the contract."

"Of course." Rake tried to swallow and struggled to find enough saliva. "Do I get to shower first?"

The doctor nodded. "The shower is right over there," he indicated, "and the change of clothes you left is in the locker."

"Great, thanks," the cloned man managed to rasp.

"Disorientation is common following the memory flash process," the doctor said. "I'll give you a few minutes to get your bearings before we begin the quality assurance process."

Rake stumbled his way to the shower and, as the water began pouring over him, realized for the first time he was completely naked. As he tried to wash the sticky red nutrient fluid from his body, he found his hair was longer than he preferred, and the stubble of a beard roughened his cheeks. *What do you expect, that they're giving you regular shaves and haircuts?* he chided himself. *When I get out of here, I'll need to find a razor.*

He steadfastly ignored the most important question, the query that kept nagging at him as his mind steadily cleared. *How did I get here? What mess did I get myself into?*

The steaming hot shower was a luxury he hadn't had in quite a while - water was scarce and jealously hoarded aboard starships, and he seldom set foot on a planet for long. While he wouldn't normally spend much time bathing, the hot water seemed to help his mind clear. *And, after all, I paid a lot of money for this policy. I might as well make sure I get every pence worth.*

When he at last shut off the water, Rake felt nearly normal again. It wasn't the first time he had been forced to use an insurance policy - in fact, it was the third – but the man never felt comfortable with it. *Probably because the first time was in a backwater facility run by pirates after they had tortured me to death and wanted a second shot at doing so*, he decided.

The change of clothes he left was standard fare - dark trousers, soft mid-calf leather boots, a light shirt, gunbelt, and a dark brown leather jacket. Concealed within the jacket was his backup handgun: heavy enough to be easy to shoot, not too heavy to aim, and completely illegal inside the cloning facility. He looked it over and decided not to push his luck, slipping it back into concealment in the jacket's lining rather than attaching it to his hip. He slipped his gunbelt on last, tightening it down and leaving the holster empty.

Harder to get at my pistol this way, but if I want to renew my policy here, I'd rather they don't *throw me out for breaking the rules.*

It was one of the few universally-accepted rules at life insurance facilities across the Colonies - no weapons inside. When the practice was first implemented, it had been an early liability problem. Growing clones and flashing memories, not to mention the necessary storage for both, were delicate and expensive processes. A freshly-decanted clone getting shot as it stepped out of its tube raised serious liability questions: was the company responsible for another clone, or had it done due diligence? Rather than debate the issue in court, insurance companies as a whole had declared their facilities weapons-free.

Carrying the pistol in his jacket lining made it harder to draw in an emergency, so Rake made a mental note to ensure the weapon was at-hand before he stepped out of the facility. *Once I'm on the street, all bets are off.*

Fully dressed and far more comfortable now that he was armed and clothed, he stepped out of the bathing facility and walked back toward where Doctor Valance was hunched over a display, no doubt with Rake's personal records and the information for his physical and mental tests.

"As you should be well aware, Mr. Weston," the doctor said without looking up, "we take quality assurance very seriously. Should this body fail to meet the necessary standards, we will need to eliminate it and grow you a new body from scratch. It will, of course, delay your departure by approximately two days, but it's a necessary precaution."

Rake tried to suppress his shudder. *So, if I fail, they kill me and start again.* He resisted the urge to flee the facility. *Then again, dead and alive again would be better than trapped in a defective body. And the general quality of this whole process has gone way, way up in the last ten years.*

"If you'll step over here, Mr. Weston, we'll begin," the doctor said with a gesture. "We'll start with reflexes, followed by a memory test, and finish with a stress test to ensure all bodily functions are working as expected."

The man reluctantly stepped over to the simulation pod for his reflexes test. With an uneasy sigh, he slipped into the seat and reached out to grasp the flight yoke for the simulator and waited for the screens to light up. The pod slid shut around him, concealing him in darkness for long moments before the displays began to illuminate.

Quality assurance was a simple process for life insurance. Three tests were run on the cloned body - memory, reflex, and stress. Each time a policyholder updated his stored memories - or "memory flashes" - the tests were run on the holder's body at that time to ensure the comparison results were current. To pass quality assurance, he had to pass each of the tests with 98% of his "baseline" from the most recent flashing. Anything less, and his current body would be eliminated and a new one would be grown for the next attempt. Cloned bodies were too prone to degenerative orders, particularly in the nervous system, to allow anything more lenient.

Rake had no particular desire to die again - plenty of motivation to put his best effort into the test.

The simulator flared to life, and he was at the controls of a starship navigating the junk fields in orbit around Earth. It was a classic reflexes simulation, designed to ensure a pilot's reflexes were up to the task of quickly responding to changing flight conditions. *This is old hat after earning my wings the first time, and then training as a pilot during the Great War*, he told himself.

The simulated ship was a small, one-man craft designed for tight and quick maneuvers. Rake remembered, very briefly, his last run in the simulation - nearly nine minutes of precision maneuvers before he had been clipped by a centuries-old satellite that ripped a wing off the ship and sent it spiraling into atmosphere.

This time, as he plunged into the debris field, he didn't feel his usual ease at the controls of a ship. Sweat began to bead on his forehead and run down into his eyes as he struggled to keep the little ship from crashing. He wove in and out of wrecked starships, shattered orbital bases, old satellites, and unidentifiable junk. Instead of relaxing, as he normally did in such a simulation, he found himself growing more and more distressed.

And then, as he ducked around a battered freighter, he saw it coming toward him like a missile: an old airlock door, three-inch alloy designed to take a military-grade explosive. He tried to shove the yoke forward and dive out of the way, but his muscles seemed to fight him. The little ship's nose pushed down, but far too slowly. A heartbeat later, the door ripped across the top of the vessel, splitting it open as neatly as a knife slicing flesh.

The simulation screens immediately went black, leaving only his time on the screen: four minutes, four seconds.

Shit.

The canopy hissed open, and Rake swallowed hard before forcing himself to look up at Doctor Valance. The man's expression was grim. "I'm sorry, Mr. Weston."

"Give me another shot at the sim," Rake said immediately. "It was bad luck, and I got blindsided. Let me have another run."

"Mr. Weston, we monitor more than just your flight time," the doctor said gently. "Your reflex time to object within line-of-sight and your reaction time to it indicate you were responding at approximately 93% of baseline."

"Give me another chance," Rake demanded through gritted teeth.

"I apologize, Mr. Weston," the doctor said as he leveled a small, handheld device at Rake - a neurostunner, useful only at ranges of a half-meter or less. "We'll have to revisit our records and see what went wrong with the first attempt. I assure you we will get the next body right, or we will refund fifty percent of the fee."

Rake reached into his jacket lining, fumbling for his gun. *I don't want to die!* he thought irrationally, knowing full well the company wouldn't just leave him dead. *I'll deal with this body!*

The doctor froze as a quiet "crack" split the air. Rake tried to draw back, knowing there was no avoiding the neurostunner.

Then the man in the white coat collapsed.

Rake stared wide-eyed at the body of the doctor as he finally withdrew his sidearm from his jacket lining. *What? What happened to...?*

"Nice and easy, Weston," a mechanically-filtered voice said coldly. "Just step out of the simulator so we can have a nice talk. Try anything stupid and, well, I doubt you've got another insurance policy ready to go."

II

RAKE GRIPPED HIS PISTOL FIRMLY, telling himself, *No, I'm not terrified. Just because there's someone out there apparently willing to break the rules to get at me doesn't mean I'm a dead man.*

Yet.

"Come on, Weston, I don't have all day," the filtered voice said.

"Who are you?" Rake demanded, checking his ammunition and charge on the weapon. *Looks good. Keep him talking, and then jump out and nail him by surprise.* He did his best to ignore the nagging voice pointing out his reflexes had already proven to be subpar.

"Does it matter, Rake? You're my payday, regardless of who I am."

"Well, you broke all the rules by coming into an insurance facility with gun in hand and you're apparently willing to shoot anyone in your way," Rake commented as he tried to recreate the room in his mind. *If he's near the entrance to this room, there's no real cover there. This simulator's on the opposite side of the room, and there's good cover here. I should be able to get a clean shot at him.* "That means you're either new to the game or damned good."

The filtered voice took on a dry tone. "My name is Slade."

Rake swallowed hard. *Great. One of the best skiptracers in the Expanse.*

"I'll admit, I thought I had you on Gallos," Slade commented. "I could have sworn no one else was even close to you. But then I find out you never even *went* to Gallos, and you turn up dead, and I had to lay down a lot of credits to find out where I could catch up with you again. Of course, now you don't have all the information that made you so valuable, but I'm sure we can find some way of getting that again."

"I'm sure," Rake repeated. "What information did I have, anyway?"

Slade's chuckle was colder than deep space. "See, that's the problem with your insurance policy. You got yourself killed, and you don't even know what's coming for—"

Rake didn't bother listening to the rest, hurling himself from the simulator and twisting his gun hand toward the entrance. His finger was squeezing the trigger when he smashed into the floor.

No Slade.

"You're not bad, kid," an unfiltered male voice said as a cold barrel tapped his ear. "Now drop the weapon."

Rake carefully laid the weapon down on the floor. "Look, I don't know what you want from me, skip, but we both know I don't have it."

"What I *want* is your head," Slade said calmly. "Now stand up."

Rake glared at the treacherous door. "You hijacked a soundbox for your voice, didn't you? So I'd be looking the wrong direction."

"Kid, you don't get to be the best by using insurance policies," Slade said smugly. "Now stand up, nice and slow, and we'll both get out of here without your insurance company paying for another body."

Rake swallowed hard. *Great. Trapped in a faulty body and caught by a skiptracer. This day couldn't get any better.* Slowly, he rose to his feet with both hands held away from his body. "I don't suppose there's any way you and I could discuss an alternative, is there?"

"Weston, a skiptracer gets a reputation by bringing in his target," the hunter said coolly. "Even if you had an extra couple million credits in your back pocket - which I somehow doubt - I wouldn't ruin my reputation by taking your money and defaulting on my contract."

Rake tried to think, but everything had moved so *fast* since he woke up in the tank. "It doesn't really have to be this way," he said offhandedly. "I mean, it's not like anyone would know."

"I shot a few of this company's staff on the way in, and I don't doubt my face is plastered all over security cameras right now. So move." He prodded the pilot again with his gun.

Rake spun, hand flashing out to knock the weapon away. Slade was caught off-guard by the sudden move and lost his grip on his carbine, allowing the two-handed gun to clatter to the floor. Rake scooped up his pistol and sprinted straight for the exit, not bothering to turn back and fire at the skiptracer.

If he lives up to his reputation, that's the last time I'll ever take him by surprise, Rake thought as he sprinted hell-bent for freedom.

He barely broke the plane of the doorway before fire blossomed in his calf. He stumbled and went down hard, smashing head-first into the hallway wall, rebounding and landing in a heap on the floor.

Rake looked down and saw blood beginning to pool on the polished tiles.

Slade walked up to him, the carbine leveled at the fallen man the entire time. He didn't speak as he bent over to retrieve Rake's pistol, attaching it to his own belt with a magnetic *click*. "Looks like my information was wrong," he remarked. "Here I thought you'd be moving slower in that new body of yours, at least for a few days. Instead you damn near make a fool of me and get away."

"I aim to please," Rake mumbled, trying to cope with the ringing in his ears, the dizziness from running headfirst into a wall, and the throbbing in his calf. "You shot me in the back. Not very professional of you."

"I shot you in the leg while you were fleeing," Slade corrected him. "Very professional of me. Prevented your escape, and I can deliver you intact to Colonel Velles."

Colonel Velles? Why does that name...? Oh, shit.

That's not good.

"Great," Rake said. "Very professional, then. Except now I can't walk out of here."

The bounty hunter looked him over, and for the first time Rake got a good close look at the infamous skiptracer.

If Slade had a last name, Rake had never heard it - and he looked like a man who didn't care about such trivial things. His dark hair was gathered back in a ponytail, and he wore a dark leather duster over a heavy set of armor. His face was unremarkable, revealing cold blue eyes, an over-large nose, and a plethora of scars.

Slade looked every bit the fearsome skiptracer his reputation made him out to be.

The armed man snorted in disgust. "Thought you were supposed to be tough, Weston. One little bullet wound and you're too injured to walk." He reached under his duster and withdrew a small coil of rope. With practiced ease he formed a loop and pulled it over Rake's uninjured leg. He pulled it tight, wrapped the other end of the rope around his left hand, and began dragging the pilot across the polished floor.

"You can't really think," Rake said from the floor as he slid along surprisingly easily, "that you're going to drag me to wherever your ship is moored."

"Hardly," Slade said. "My AI and my ship are already at the emergency docking collar at the hospital across the walkway. In a few minutes you'll be locked away until I can get you to Velles."

Rake considered his options. *Well, I can try to fight him with a bad leg while my good leg is bound, and I'm completely unarmed. Or I can let him drag me to his ship and try to escape from him there, also while injured and unarmed.*

I don't like either of these options.

The hallways of the insurance facility were empty of the living as Slade stalked through them, dragging his prey behind like Rake was already dead. Dead men and women were scattered across the floor, Rake's clothes soaking and darkening as he was dragged through the pools of blood. Still, no one attempted to intercept the skiptracer, and frustration started to well up in the bound man's chest.

I hate the Core worlds. Earth or Terra VI, they're both alike. Well, they were before Earth cooked. Everyone's too damned scared to do anything, Rake thought distastefully. *They all forget how to fight when they need it. This skiptracer walked into their facility, shot a bunch of 'em, and drags a client out by a leg, and they just sit around and wait for the law to get here.*

Figures.

The front door to the insurance facility hissed open, allowing Slade to walk out with his bound captive in his wake. He immediately turned hard to his left and didn't miss a step, even when Rake bounced off the corner of the door.

"Ow," the pilot complained. "Keep that up, and you won't be bringing me back in working order."

"Shut up," Slade said.

With nothing else to say, Rake found himself complying, even as he tried to find a way out of the trap he was caught in. Nothing brilliant came to mind.

The insurance facility and the hospital, separated by less than fifty meters of walkway, were both against the edge of the Terra VI orbital station to better allow for emergency access. Two airlocks were available in the space, allowing for a pair of ships to be offloaded at the same time. Both locks were currently occupied, the vessels partially visible through the transparent alloy commonly installed in viewports on space-going vessels; the skiptracer was clearly making his way for the lock closer to the insurance facility.

If he gets me on his ship, I'm dead, Rake thought bleakly. *Wow. What a wonderful investment the life insurance policy was this time. I would've been better off staying dead.*

They were ten meters away from the lock when Slade's ship blew up.

The viewport took the blast without so much as a scratch - it was actually tougher than the far less expensive materials used to build ship hulls - but the open airlock wasn't so fortunate. As the remains of the ship were hurled out into open space, the damaged lock failed to close.

Wind, virtually unheard of aboard space stations, quickly rose to a howl as it rushed out the compromised portal.

Aboard a station this size, the chances of the airlock failure being fatal to the inhabitants was minimal - it would take many minutes to empty the atmosphere into vacuum from such a large space. However, that was the concern furthest from either of their minds.

Slade swore, a curse Rake had never heard before. "Vultures!" he shouted. "Always some damned vultures around to steal the prize!"

Chips of flooring began to fly up as bullets rattled around them. Slade took a pair of them without so much as a grunt - his partly-concealed armor deflected the projectiles - but scrambled to free his breathing mask from his belt.

A figure in an assault suit stepped through the compromised airlock. Rake stared in disbelief. *That takes guts.* The newcomer leveled his weapon and let another burst loose at Slade. *To come in that fast, he had to be sitting just about on top of Slade's ship when it blew up. That assault suit can take a few bullets without venting into space, but shrapnel could have taken it to pieces.*

Another trio of bullets smacked into the skiptracer. He swore again and dropped the rope around Rake's uninjured right leg. Slade's hands ducked under his duster and came out with a pair of pistols, firing nearly non-stop toward the attacker as he half-ran for the scarce cover of a parked magnetic transport car.

Rake decided this was the moment he was looking for and ran for his life.

Or he would have, had his leg not had a neat hole poked through it.

"Rake, come on!" the newcomer shouted, his voice as mechanically filtered as Slade's had been in the testing room. "Come on, we have to get out of here!"

Try to get away from them both with an injured leg and take my chances getting caught by Slade again, or go with the person I don't know? With his calf throbbing, there wasn't much of a choice. *There's no reward without risk.*

He crawled as quickly as he could for the newcomer.

"Dammit, Rake, run!" the attacker shouted.

Deciding that some forward motion was better than none, Rake elected to continue crawling.

The angry whine of bullets over his head motivated him to do better, and a glance over his shoulder confirmed that Slade, rather than risk losing his prey, had chosen to shoot him, too. Doing his best to ignore the pain, Rake forced himself unsteadily to his feet and ran as best he could, his leg on fire every step of the way to the airlock.

Slade wasn't going to let him go that easily, though.

The skiptracer was on the move again, this time with a different weapon in his right hand - a highly illegal, very powerful, and very difficult-to-aim rocket pistol.

The newcomer apparently saw it, too. "Into the airlock," he shouted frantically to Rake. "Now!"

Hobbled by his injury, Rake knew he wouldn't make it - not when his leg gave out again and he crashed to the deck.

Slade leveled the weapon.

The newcomer dove to the ground.

And a new roar joined the rushing wind.

Metal shrapnel sprayed out at Rake. None of it was life-threatening; the pieces were small and tumbling, though several of them flayed his arms open even through his jacket as he cradled his own head.

The tortured scream of punctured, stressed metal and the ever-increasing roar of wind battled for supremacy for several seconds, before the metal surrendered the contest. Rake looked up, not understanding what had happened.

Holes as large as his fist had been punched through the station's exterior. Rake's eyes widened. *That other ship at the hospital airlock...was shooting at Slade? A starship, trying to shoot a person?* The roar in his ears continued to grow in strength. *And might have killed us all.*

Then there were arms lifting him. Dizziness began to sweep over him. *Hypoxia*, he thought. *The air's moving past me too fast to get proper oxygen.*

As his consciousness faded, he managed one last thought: *I didn't have time to take out another policy.*

III

RAKE TRIED TO OPEN HIS eyes, but light stabbed him viciously. He immediately squeezed his eyelids shut again for a few moments before he tried again, this time more slowly. The light was merciless, but he persisted against the pain.

Did I die again? he wondered, then immediately dismissed the notion. *No, if I had died again, I'd remember getting another insurance policy. Last thing I remember is that skiptracer, and a shootout, and the air venting into space. If I were dead, they'd have used my memories from before to bring me back, and I wouldn't remember the shootout.*

He congratulated himself on his reasoning. *So, I'm okay. But where am I?*

The light finally seemed to ease its attack, and Rake slowly soaked in the details as they came into focus. The overhead lights hung from a metal ceiling, gently curving toward the floor. He was lying on a surgical table of some sort, with a medical AI standing nearby in a powered-off state. A single viewport looked out into the darkness of space, providing an unparalleled view of brilliant stars.

Cabinets lined the walls, all the workspaces clear of any loose items. Rake lifted his arms and found he was just barely bound - only a simple harness to keep him safe while unconscious, and it released at the touch of a finger. He did some more mental math. *Okay, so everything's neatly stored away and tidy as can be. Between that and the view of the stars, I must be on a ship. Given the firefight outside the insurance facility, it's probably the ship that shot the place up. And given that I'm not tied down, they're probably not skiptracers, either.*

Someone rescued me.

Rake slowly sat up, giving himself time to adjust. Dizziness swept over him, but he refused to relent. When he was fully sitting up, he slowly pulled himself around to let his legs dangle off the bed. Taking his time, he eased himself off, carefully transferring his weight to his feet, supporting himself with his arms to ensure he didn't fall.

It wasn't until he was standing with most of his weight on his legs that he realized he wasn't feeling any pain from his wounded leg. He looked down in surprise and saw clean white medical wrapping securely in place around his entire calf, from knee to ankle. He experimentally shifted even more of his weight to his wounded leg and felt barely a twinge from it. *Definitely not skiptracers*, he decided. *They wouldn't have bothered patching me up unless it was a critical wound and they needed me alive for the reward.*

As he straightened up, no longer leaning on the bed, he had another sudden revelation: he was dressed only in a thin medical gown. Rake glanced around, but saw no sign of his clothes. "Of course not," he muttered. "With everything else packed away, they would have packed my clothes up, too. No loose objects on a ship."

A wolf whistle from the door brought Rake's head up and around. Leaning against the frame, arms crossed, was a gorgeous dark-haired woman, hair cropped well above her shoulders and hanging loosely around her heart-shaped face. "I think I prefer to keep you like this."

"Like this?" Rake repeated.

"Mostly naked," the woman said with a wink.

"Uh, right," Rake muttered, blushing before he could catch himself. "It seems you have me at a disadvantage," he answered. "If we're going to be on equal footing, maybe you should strip down, too."

She laughed, a wicked sound promising all sorts of delights. "Who said I want to be equal with you?" She finally relented with a brilliant smile. "Check the upper drawer under the bed."

Rake bent over and pulled the drawer open, finding it empty. He looked up questioningly at the woman.

Her smile was just as wicked as before. "Oops, my mistake. One drawer lower."

The man glanced down at himself and realized the gown had ridden up when he had bent over. He blushed again, then shrugged and pulled open the lower drawer.

He found his clothes neatly folded inside - the trousers, shirt, gunbelt, and jacket he'd worn in the insurance facility, thankfully free of blood. Gratefully, he pulled the clothes out and started dressing, pulling on the pants before he shed the medical gown.

"You don't need to do that," she said lightly. "After all, it's nothing I haven't seen already."

"I'll keep that in mind," Rake said dryly as he pulled his shirt over his head. "Quite the voyeur, are you?"

"Fine way to talk to the woman who pulled your ass out of the fire," she said, her light tone contrasting her words. "Next time a skiptracer has you, I'm just going to watch."

Rake raised an eyebrow at her as he pulled his jacket on. "Wait, that was *you* shooting at Slade?"

The woman raised both eyebrows in return. "That skiptracer was *Slade?!*"

"You didn't know?" Rake asked in return.

"Honey, when I got your message to pick you up from the insurance facility, I had no idea you were in *that* kind of trouble." She shook her head. "Damn, that was an enemy I could have happily never made."

"Pick me up?" His head was spinning. "I'm out of it for a few weeks, and nothing makes sense."

The woman offered him another dazzling smile. "You don't even recognize me, do you, Rake?"

The question set him aback. "I know you?"

She shook her head. "For shame, Rake. If your stored memories are *that* old, we're never going to get you clear of this mess you're in."

Rake studied her for a moment, and then a moment longer before he finally recognized the dark blue eyes nearly hidden behind the dark hair. "I'll be damned," he breathed. "Caree Staka."

"Ah, you *do* remember me. I was prepared to be offended," she said with a wink.

"How many years has it been since you and I pulled that job off New Recice?" Rake asked with a shake of his head. "We were both still wet-behind-the-ears kids!"

Caree grinned. "That didn't stop us from doing some stupid things," she said.

"It's probably *why* we did stupid things," Rake replied with a broad smile of his own.

"Aw, is that the only reason we…?"

"Hell, no," he interrupted. "If that was the only reason, you think I would call you because I'm in trouble?"

"Always the charmer, Rake. You haven't changed a bit."

"*You* have," he commented. When she raised an eyebrow, he added, "You're all the more beautiful for it. Besides, the Caree I worked with off New Recice would never have walked into the middle of a shooting match."

"I did no such thing," she sniffed disdainfully. "I *started* that fight."

"So, uh," Rake said awkwardly, "if you have some idea what's going on, I'd love to know. I kind of woke up from a tank and have no idea what I've gotten myself into."

Caree grimaced. "I was hoping you took a flash of your memories before you died so that you would know."

"Well, what *do* you know?" he asked. "How did you know where to find me, or even that I needed help?"

The dark-haired beauty blew out a sigh. "Of course, on to business."

"Sorry."

"No, it's okay." She shrugged, a liquid motion that drew Rake's eyes. "I've just…missed you." She held up a hand to forestall his reply. "Business first."

"So, first question," Rake said. "Where are we?"

"Edge of the Terra system," was Caree's answer. "We're mostly powered down, passive sensors only, and our core is cool enough that we should be invisible against background noise unless someone's running active scans. And if they are, we'll pick them up with the passives."

"And if we need to run, how long will it take you to be ready?" he asked with a raised eyebrow.

"We've already got an emergency jump plotted," she said. "We've got enough power in the capacitors to hit the point drive, but we'll have nothing left when we get there."

"That's a *lot* of juice in the caps," Rake commented. "Bit past spec, isn't it?"

She smiled. "Since when are *you* concerned with safety?"

Instead of answering, he changed the subject. "So how did you find me? And why were you out here in the first place?"

Caree paused for a moment before answering. "Just over three days ago, I got a transmission from you out at Clarion. You wouldn't give me the details, but you said you were in a lot of trouble and didn't think you'd survive. You told me you had a life insurance policy at one of the Terra insurance companies and you'd need me to pick you up in a few days if things went south." She grimaced. "You told me you needed someone you could trust if you were going to slip the skiptracers chasing you, and that you'd need to lay low for a while."

"With the mess we left on that station, I'd say I was right," Rake grumbled. "So I didn't tell you anything more? Any hint at what kind of trouble I was in?"

She shook her head. "Not a word, other than to say how bad it was."

"Well, at least one skip figured out I had a life insurance policy," he said grimly. "Not only that, but he figured out where they'd be bringing me off ice. And where there's one, there will be more." Rake contemplated for a moment before asking, "So where are we headed?"

"I was hoping you would have an answer for that question. I came all the way to Terra to get you - we had no job that would've taken us this close to *civilization*," she said, adding a slight mocking tone to the final word.

"Let me think on it a bit," Rake said. "Actually, no need to think about it." He took a deep breath. "Set a course for Clarion."

Caree stared at him. "Um, wouldn't that be where you were killed? Are you sure no one is going to still be looking for you there?"

The pilot shook his head. "I died a few days ago, and word officially made it onto the ComNet if my insurance policy was invoked. Anyone who was looking for me there will know I'm dead and gone." He offered a cynical smile. "In fact, they're probably combing Earth, Terra, and the rest of the Home Region, waiting for me to show up at an insurance company."

The woman paled. "So it would probably be best to get us out of the Home Region," she said.

Rake nodded. "Clarion."

She frowned at him, but the expression didn't detract a shred from her beauty, which Rake was trying very hard to ignore. "What are you hoping to find there?"

"Two things," Rake answered. "First, maybe I can kick up something to tell me *why* skiptracers were hunting me down with intention to kill. And second, I want my ship back. I'd bet every credit I have left that my ship is parked somewhere in that system."

"Pilots," she murmured. "You're all alike."

He snorted. "What does that make you?"

Caree offered another dazzling smile. "I'm the captain, not the pilot."

"Well, then, *captain*, you'd best give the orders to get us moving," Rake said with a broad smile and a nod.

"Of course," she said with just a bit of stiffness. "I'll be back in a few minutes, once we have this boat under way."

Rake watched her leave, admiring her backside the whole time. When she had disappeared from sight, he forced himself to sit down and think.

Okay, Rake, he told himself, *start from what you know. First, you know you died sometime in the last few days. Your death was reported on the ComNet, and your life insurance policy brought this body off ice with your last memories restored. Sometime between that flash two weeks ago and the day you were killed, you got yourself into some kind of trouble - something deep. You were killed, most likely on Clarion, but that didn't satisfy whoever was after you, since a skiptracer showed up here at Terra to try to grab you.*

Not only that, but he did it inside an insurance facility. That realization worried him. *Not only was this something bad enough to get you shot, but it was bad enough for a skiptracer to break all rules of decorum to make sure you didn't make it out of the facility before catching you. The credit payout on your head must be* huge. *Large enough to risk breaking dozens of laws to get.*

Well, at least I know I'm not wanted by any of the Home Region governments. He smiled to himself. *They would've had uniformed officers there to arrest me, not some skiptracer.*

I must be in trouble on one of the Outlying Worlds, or with one of the kingpins. Of course, Colonel Velles is also looking for me, if I take Slade's word for it, but that doesn't make any sense - why would the Terran military hire a skiptracer instead of doing the job themselves?

Rake frowned. *This business doesn't lead to a lot of friends, but I must not have thought I could trust anyone if I called Caree to pick me up. We haven't spoken in years, but she was always as good as her word.*

The pilot continued to sit with eyes closed as he continued to poke and prod at the few facts he knew, trying to wring out any more information, but they were as dry as stones.

Even with the distraction of his own thoughts, and the deep-seated fear underlying them, he couldn't miss the sensation of a point-to-point jump.

Rake didn't understand exactly how point drives worked - for that matter, he doubted more people than a handful of astrophysicists in the entire Expanse truly understood it. The usual metaphor for the technology was enough to satisfy his need for knowledge.

Developed several centuries ago, point drives were the solution to the speed-of-light limit. Instead of hurling a craft at transluminal velocities - long discovered impossible - point drives bent space itself to allow immediate transition from one spot to the next. When Rake was a child, he had been taught the concept with a single sheet of paper. If a person lived on that paper, in two dimensions, he'd never experience the third dimension that was being bent. When the paper met, he might be able to pop from one half of the sheet to the other, without actually crossing the open paper between the two points.

Point drives had major drawbacks. Properly calculating a point-to-point jump was nearly impossible, because the calculations required knowing about every single mass object larger than a few specks of dust between a ship's current position and its intended destination, as those objects affected how space "folded".

Because of the sheer complexity of it, all ships except exploration craft were limited to pre-existing transition points, and point drive exploration had been dead for nearly twenty years - the war between Earth and Terra had seen to that. Short jumps were simple enough to calculate, even by hand, but long-distance travel was dangerous and complicated outside of the known jumps.

And there was always the effect point-to-point travel had on humans.

A quarter of humans weren't affected at all, but for the rest of humanity, using the point drives was an uncomfortable experience.

Rake always likened the sensation to being ripped away, completely disoriented, and then dropped in a new place. As a pilot, he had a fairly keen sense of direction and could virtually always keep his bearings, but jumps left him dizzy for half a minute or so.

This jump was no better. In fact, it was much worse.

Rake woke up on the deck of the medical bay, staring up at the light overhead. An ache at the back of his head pounded in time with his heartbeat.

"Ow," he muttered. "Well, that was ugly."

"Rake?" a voice called on the medical bay's intercom. "Rake, are you still there?"

He pulled himself to his feet, using both hands to keep himself steady. "I'm here, Caree."

"I was hoping to hear that," she said with a bit of strain in her voice. "We're being hailed, and they're looking for you."

IV

THE BRIDGE OF CAREE'S SHIP was already crowded when Rake stepped up through the hatchway.

Caree herself stood in the middle of the bridge. Rake glanced around, soaking in the details. *She's standing because she has no command seat*, he noted with some surprise. *Only seats available are the pilot's chair and the navigation chair, and the jump chairs at the back of the bridge.*

Both the aforementioned stations were occupied - the pilot's chair by a dark-skinned man built like he came from a high gravity world, the navigator's chair by a pale girl with nearly-white hair that looked far too young to be voyaging into the space lanes. *She can't be more than fifteen years old, by Earth standards*, he thought in dismay.

Two more crewman stood at the back of the bridge, a man and a woman with similar bright ice-blue eyes under dark hair. *Brother and sister*, Rake guessed. *And, unless I'm completely wrong, that should be Caree's entire crew.*

"Captain Staka," Rake said, keeping his voice even. *No sense causing any trouble for her with the crew*, he decided immediately. *So keep it professional.*

"It appears you have some friends, Rake," she said lightly, but there was an undertone of tension in her voice. "Some more friends, I should say. They've been asking very politely if you're on board."

"And what have you been telling them?" he asked with a raised eyebrow.

"We haven't officially replied to their query yet," she said with a smile. "Until we figure out *how* to answer."

"So who's doing the asking?" Rake wanted to know.

The gorgeous captain reached up and pulled down two screens from the ceiling. She impatiently tapped the corner of one of the screens, until at last it yielded up images of two patrol craft. "These are your friends," she commented. "They're bearing the colors and identification codes for local militia."

"What's local?" Rake asked.

"What, did you forget your navigation charts?" Caree responded. "We're in the Lantash system."

"Lantash?" he repeated. "That's hardly the first jump toward Clarion."

"It's the long way around," the captain agreed, "but if you died on Clarion, and your policy was cashed in at one of the Terra facilities, skiptracers are probably going to be watching the usual routes. It'll take more fuel, but it should have kept us from getting caught."

"Except it didn't."

"Except it didn't," Caree agreed. "They must want you *bad.*"

"You think they already know I'm alive?" Rake asked.

"Maybe. From what I know of Slade, he was probably working solo, but it looks like they're covering all the bases to try to grab you."

Rake decided to change the subject. "What are those patrol ships packing?"

Caree tapped at the second screen. When it didn't respond, she banged it with her fist in annoyance. After another moment, streaks of red overlaid the diagnostic of the patrol boat.

Rake stepped forward to get a better look at the screen. The vessel was a sloop - hardly considered a capital ship by modern standards. At a hundred meters long, it packed two dozen small-caliber coilguns highlighted in red on the diagram, which would be plenty against any freighters or pirate ships plying the space lanes. A trio of powerful engines could propel it at decent acceleration, and a point drive allowed for intersystem travel. The whole vessel was vaguely wedge-shaped with smooth, flat surfaces, a typical design for a warship: it allowed for high-firepower, low-profile edges to point at an enemy.

"How many guns does your ship have?" Rake asked quietly.

"The *Starfall* isn't a warship," Caree reprimanded him. "I can't go to guns with two of those patrol boats - they'll tear us to shreds."

"How many gees can you pull?" was his next question.

"Running?" Caree raised an eyebrow at him, then looked at the diagrams. "They'll take us to pieces before we can get out of range."

"I have a hunch about that," Rake said. "But we can outrun them?"

The captain nodded. "Yes, we can pull a lot more gees than they can."

The navigator spoke up. "If we try to run, cap, we're going to wind up stranded."

Caree looked over at the white-haired girl. "Again?"

"We won't have enough fuel for a jump if we run the engines for a long burn," she explained. "There's no way we could head back to Terra or continue on to Clarion without refueling."

"So why didn't you let me know we needed refueling?" the captain asked.

"Cap, we were going to refuel at one of the Terra stations," the pilot interjected. "You told us it was going to be a simple pickup, and we'd have a few days in system."

"Damn," Caree muttered. "Damn, damn, damn. We're caught because we're out of gas."

The navigator nodded. "We can outrun them, but wherever we choose to set down to refuel, we'll light up their sensors like a candle."

"Wait," Rake interjected. "You just mean re-entry, right? That everyone will know we're there from the fire?"

"Right. No need for fancy sensors or spaceport controls, just the physical signs we'll be giving off," she affirmed.

"Can you bring me up a system map?" Rake asked Caree.

The captain frowned but turned her attention back to the secondary screen again. Several irritated taps later, the image of the patrol sloop vanished to be replaced by a map of the star system. "Not to scale, of course."

"Of course," Rake murmured as he studied the display.

At the center was, of course, the system's sun. The two planets orbiting closest were both colonized and boasted first-class starport facilities, capable of accommodating ships even larger than the patrol sloops and refueling any vessel short of a nuclear-powered cruiser. The third and fourth worlds were small, cold rocks incapable of hosting life. The fifth world was partly terraformed, but the process had been left incomplete by the Great War. The sixth planet was a ringed gas giant, while the seventh and last world was so small it was hardly considered a planet at all.

"This is perfect," he murmured. "Lantash Six is the closest world."

Caree frowned at him. "Lantash Six? It's a gas giant. We can't land there - the atmosphere is so dense it would crush us like a bug before we made it to the ground."

"Which is why it's perfect." Rake glanced at the navigator. "Do we have enough fuel for an in-system jump?"

"Yes, but it doesn't change the fact that we need to land to refuel," the girl replied. "There's no orbital stations for us to dock."

"You're right about that," Rake agreed. "Do we have the power to run now?"

Caree glanced over at the pilot. "Wings?"

The dark-skinned man - Wings, apparently - glanced over his own status screens before answering. "Yes," he answered. "Our engines are warmed up and ready after the cold jump from Terra."

"What's your plan, Weston?" the captain asked him.

Rake tapped the display. "Are you familiar with the rings of Lantash Six?"

"I'm guessing there's something I don't know about there?" she asked instead of answering.

The man nodded. "Something, yes." He tapped the display. "Put in a direct course for Lantash Two, full burn. As soon as you have the point drive spooled up, we jump straight to Lantash Six, as close as you can manage. It'll throw the patrol boats off."

"That'll just burn up more of our fuel," the navigator protested.

"Trust me." Rake offered a confident smile.

"This is crazy, cap," the girl said, looking past the passenger.

Caree slowly began to smile. "Lay in the course," she said. "And start the calculations."

"Cap," Wings protested, "when I light the engines, those patrol boats are going to light us up."

"No, they won't," the dark-haired woman said. "They're hunting our friend here. Judging by that skiptracer back on Terra, I'd guess they want him alive. They won't risk blowing us up."

"They don't know he's on board," one of the siblings said from the back of the bridge. "We haven't replied."

"Is our course laid in?" Caree asked.

Both pilot and navigator nodded.

"Get ready to punch up a full burn," the captain ordered. "And everyone strap in. You too, Rake."

As Rake strapped into one of the jump seats lining the back wall, Caree dragged one of the screens to the back of the bridge with her. The display hung up at one point until she jerked it, freeing it again to slide aft until it hung in front of Rake's chair. The captain strapped herself in beside the fugitive, then slid the screen over until both of them could see it.

"Caree?" he murmured.

She grinned at him. "Trust me." She reached out and touched the display and, for once, it responded immediately. The system map vanished, replaced by the image of a man in a uniform. "This is Captain Staka aboard the *Starfall*," she announced. "I have Rake Weston on board." She grinned. "Catch us if you can."

The ship seemed to leap out from under Rake as Wings punched in the full burn. He didn't have time to contemplate it, though, as the monitor smashed into his chest, thrown into him by the massive acceleration. The very chair he was sitting in vibrated with the rumble of the vessel's engines.

He could feel shards of glass jabbing into his chest and guessed the screen had shattered under the impact. With an effort, he glanced over and saw Caree was similarly grimacing under the pressure. "I forgot," she muttered with an effort. "This is exactly what happened last time."

"Last time?" Rake managed. "You do this often?"

The freighter bucked, hard, but the crew was all firmly strapped in. "We're taking fire!" the girl at navigation shouted.

"If they wanted us dead, our hull would already be full of holes," Caree grunted. "They're making a show to try to get us to surrender."

"Ready to jump at any time, cap," Wings called.

"Don't wait on account of me," the woman answered.

There was another gut-wrenching jerk, and then Rake felt as though his bearings were again entirely stripped away. It wasn't as bad this time - he didn't lose consciousness. Nausea swept over him, but he managed to keep from retching as the ship vanished from one location and appeared in another.

The roar of the engines fell away, and the ship quit shaking a few moments later. Out the viewport, Rake could see the massive, colorful swirl of Lantash Six nearby.

It was further than he thought, of course - gas giants were huge and deceptive that way.

The rings of Lantash Six were a phenomena unmatched in the Expanse. Planetary rings were normally, by and large, colorful space debris. They consisted of bits of dust and small rock and stray gases, and while solid-appearing from a distance, they were quite insubstantial while at close range. In some ways, they were as deceptive as clouds.

Except the rings of Lantash Six.

There was speculation among scientists that they had been formed of molten material ejected into orbit by a series of meteor strikes; others held that the rings were simply so ancient they had accumulated massive amounts of free-floating space debris. In either case, the rings of Lantash Six were utterly unique.

They were solid, unbroken, fused stone.

And they were barely five hundred meters away from the *Starfall*.

Wings yelped in surprise. "Plotted that one a bit tight, didn't you?"

Rake was pressed back into his seat as Wings applied power from the engines. The *Starfall*'s nose came up, but thousands of tons of momentum kept pushing it toward disaster. The freighter shuddered as the pilot applied full thrust, the engines roaring in response. Painfully slowly, the vessel's momentum changed, even as the vessel skimmed along the ring. Mountains thrust up like fingers, jagged from millennia without the eroding effects of wind or water. The freighter slowed as Wings applied counterthrust, using every technique he had to avoid disaster.

There was a tiny "ping", barely audible over the scream of overdriven engines, and then the *Starfall* was gaining altitude, pulling away from the ring.

Rake blew out a sigh of relief. "That was too close." Then he winced as pain stabbed through his chest again. "Ow."

Caree grimaced as she pushed the broken monitor away from the two of them. "Next time, Joy, could you leave a little more margin for error?"

The girl at navigation - Joy, apparently - looked up with an abashed expression. "Sorry, Cap."

Rake shook his head. "That was *insane*. I've never seen someone plot a jump that tight."

"She's just that good," Caree said as she looked down at her bloodstained shirt. "She's a lot smarter than her captain, too." Her gaze lifted to lock with Rake's. "Since this was your idea, where to now?"

"We'll need a scan of the ring's topography," he instructed as he looked at his own blood-soaked shirt. *So much for my clothes being so nice and clean*, he thought. "We're looking for a canyon two kilometers long, with a single mountain capping either end."

"I don't have anything like that where we can see it," Joy said.

"I didn't expect us to be that lucky. We'll have to orbit until you see it."

"And what's so important about this canyon?" Wings asked.

Rake's smile was small and tight. "Back during the war, Lantash was controlled by Terra, but not all the locals liked it. The Earth loyalists set up a resistance base on the rings. Friendly forces coming through used it for refueling and repairs, and the Terrans knew it was there, but they never found it."

"But you knew where it was," Caree stated.

"Not until after," Rake said with a shake of his head. "After the war, the loyalists there turned it into a smuggler hole. Now days it's used for brokering deals and fueling ships that can't, for whatever reason, deal with the local authorities."

"Like us." Caree smiled broadly. "How did I never know about this?"

"It's not widely advertised," Rake said. "Even on the worlds I frequent. The few people that know about it have plenty of reason to keep it quiet - after all, if word got back to the officials on Lantash One, or even Terra, they'd send in a couple of frigates to clean the place out."

"So, when we find this canyon, what do we do?" Joy asked.

"I transmit the code clearance, we land, we pay exorbitant prices for fuel, and then we get the hell out," Rake said grimly.

"Great plan," Caree said. "I'll make sure we charge the fuel to your account. Come on, let's go down to the medical bay and get cleaned up. This could take a while."

She offered a small smile. "You and I have some things to talk about."

V

YOU KNOW," CAREE SAID CHEERFULLY as she slathered salve on Rake's battered chest, "I never got to ask you. Where'd you get the money for the insurance policy?"

Rake grimaced, more from the coolness of the gel than from pain. "What are you talking about?"

"I'm not a fool, Rake," she said lightly. "You've been involved in a lot of jobs in the outer worlds, including several in the zero security zone, outside civilization. You've made a name for yourself as a great pilot and a man who can think on his feet. But none of those jobs have been a big score - nothing that would've paid the millions you needed for an insurance policy."

"Oh, come on," Rake complained. "Are you really telling me you've seen my finances? You've been looking into my books?"

"No," Caree said with a shake of her head. "I don't need to do that. I *also* know what kind of lifestyle you've lived. You're burning cash like anyone living in the outer worlds. Not to mention the upgrades to your ship," she added. Then she paused. "That reminds me - do you have another insurance policy?"

Rake shook his head. "No, I don't. There was only enough cash for one."

"So where'd the money come from?"

The pilot hesitated for long moments, the silence heavy as Caree finished smearing salve and began wrapping his wounds with bandages. Finally, he said, "I don't know."

"You don't know?" she repeated skeptically.

"No. I was given a large lump of cash over a year ago, with express instructions to get a life insurance policy. I didn't question it - just made a trip to Terra and went through the process. Then, three weeks ago, I got another payment with instructions to ensure my memory was up to date - enough cash to cover the update and the trip to Terra."

"And you didn't ask where this was coming from?"

"I *did* look into it, a year ago, when I got the first payment. The money came from an account on New Persia with a name that went nowhere. I had some friends look into *that*, and the money for that account came from Earth, and the transfer date was before the Great War."

Caree grimaced. "So, no way to trace it."

"No, there's no way." No further explanation was necessary; Earth's financial records had burned with the planet.

"So, you think your mystery benefactor had something to do with your death?" Caree asked. "I mean, it's like he knew you might not make it through…whatever you got yourself into."

Rake nodded. "Good chance."

"So, that begs the question - what were you involved with a year ago? Someone apparently was making an investment then to ensure you survived."

"I'm not sure," Rake confessed.

"Why not?" Caree asked.

Rake considered his options carefully. *I really don't remember, but that might be because of this body. Or maybe it's because I really don't remember. Until I can get my ship back, and get to all my ship logs, I really don't know.*

"Most of my memories from…before…are kind of fuzzy. According to the doc on Terra, it's common after the wake up," he lied. "He said it might take a few weeks for me to recall everything clearly." *In a few weeks, I'll either be clear of this, or dead.*

"So, what's your plan?" the woman asked. "Besides get to your ship?"

The pilot slid off the bed, carefully pulling on a fresh shirt over his tender skin. "If I can find my ship, the navigation logs should tell me where I've been. Between that and my personal logs, I should be able to reconstruct what I've been doing, and hopefully pay off whatever crime boss is sending all these guys after me."

"A crime boss?" Caree was skeptical. "Those were Lantash authority sloops that shot up our tail, not pirate ships."

"A skiptracer working for the law wouldn't risk shooting up an insurance facility," Rake said firmly. "No, it has to be someone on the outer worlds - maybe even someone in the zero security zone." He raised an eyebrow. "You want some help with your wounds?"

The dark-haired beauty offered a wink before smoothly doffing her shirt. "Not the first time you've seen this, now, is it?"

Rake nearly swallowed his tongue as he picked up the can of salve. As methodically as he could manage, he carefully began rubbing in salve over her wounds. Like his own, they were small and numerous, tiny cuts that had covered her chest in a sheet of blood. With his off hand, he picked up a towel and carefully began to clean the blood from her skin as well.

"No, not the first time," he finally managed to say.

Caree offered him a teasing grin. "Pay attention to your work," she said lightly.

"Of course," he said, deciding to stay quiet and concentrate on what he was doing.

"So," she said after a few moments of silence, "what comes after you find your ship? You round up your crew and go after...whatever it is?"

"No crew," Rake said.

"No crew?" she asked in surprise. "How do you man your ship?"

The man hesitated for a moment. *How many secrets do I really want to give her?* "She's an advanced ship, designed for a minimal crew. The complement is supposed to be three, actually - a pilot, a weapons officer, and an engineer."

"And you, of course, do all three."

"I'm a man of many talents," Rake boasted.

Caree leaned forward against his hands, which were still ministering to her chest. "Yes, yes you are."

He did his best to maintain composure, but she was *very* good at distracting him. "I do my best."

"So," the dark-haired woman said after a few moments of silence, "What's the name of your ship?"

"Getting personal, are we?"

"Given our mutual lack of clothes, I'd say we're already personal, aren't we?" Caree winked.

"So do you really want to talk about my ship?" he asked dryly.

"Isn't that the way to sweet-talk you pilots?" she countered. "Talk about ships and engines and guns? I thought you'd like that kind of pillow-talk."

"We're not on a pillow," Rake deadpanned.

"Let's fix that," Caree grinned, taking his hand.

* * *

Almost eleven hours later, the intercom in Caree's cabin beeped for attention. The dark-haired woman lazily rolled off Rake's chest and stretched an arm out to tap the answer button. "Go ahead."

"Cap, we found the canyon," Wings reported. "Just like Weston described."

"Put us in stationary orbit over the canyon and wait for us," the captain ordered. "We'll be there shortly."

Wings was silent for a moment. Rake guessed he was processing the meaning of *we*. "Yes, Cap." The intercom beeped to signal the line closing.

"Guess that means we have to get up," Rake grumbled.

"Are you complaining, sweetheart?" Caree asked with a wicked grin. "Didn't get enough rest?"

"Plenty of time in bed, but not much rest," he answered lazily. "I've hardly slept since I woke up at Terra."

"Sleep when you're dead," she teased.

"Already tried that once. Wasn't restful."

Caree smacked him playfully in the shoulder. "Quit your complaining and get dressed, dead man."

* * *

It took twenty minutes of haggling over the short-range radio to secure permission to land - eight minutes of arguing over Rake's out-of-date clearance code, and another twelve minutes to settle on berthing fees that, while still high, weren't as outrageous as the initial offer. Caree had wanted to continue the negotiation, but the *Starfall*'s passive sensors had picked up faint sensor pings from one of the Lantash sloops - too weak to reveal the location of the ship, but plenty of warning that the authorities hadn't given up their search.

The landing zone was concealed at the bottom of the canyon, with no external lights or signals to betray the location. Rake had to admit that, in spite of his professional distaste for riding in a ship he wasn't flying, Wings was a pretty fair pilot. The big man slipped the freighter under the overhanging rock, putting plenty of cover between them and their pursuers.

It took another minute of careful maneuvering to mate the *Starfall's* airlock with a docking tube that extended from seemingly sheer stone wall.

As the airlock hissed open, wind blew over Rake, ruffling his too-long hair. His ears popped as the pressures equalized, and the artificial breeze died off.

Let's hope for no trouble, he thought.

The gun in his holster felt wrong. Not because Rake had any problem with carrying a handgun - especially in rat holes like the Lantash Six smuggler hole. He had carried a sidearm most of his adult life. No, the problem was that the pistol was all *wrong*. The weapon was too light, the barrel too long. The balance was entirely off, and he couldn't feel the natural point of the weapon when he swung on a target.

"No boarders?" Caree asked when the airlock and connecting tube remained empty. "I thought they'd send a welcoming party."

"No reason to bother," Rake said grimly. "Everyone inside will be armed, so if we run in guns blazing we'd be dead. They've probably got dozens of coilguns embedded in the rock pointed right at the ship. If we do anything too stupid, they'll cut the *Starfall* to shreds."

"Ah. So why, exactly, are we walking into this place?" Caree asked warily.

"This is hardly the first smuggler hole you've frequented," Rake commented. "Any place like this can't depend on local security - they're hardly going to call the Lantash authorities, are they? So they take precautions to ensure nothing too horrid happens."

Caree glanced back at her crew, gathered behind them. "So, I'd guess we should leave the crew here."

"That would be ideal. We don't want to risk starting a fight."

Caree waved off her crew. None of the four looked happy, but they retreated back into the *Starfall* as per their captain's wishes. When they had all vanished, the dark-haired woman looked over at Rake. "After you."

"Yep." Rake walked through the airlock and into the connecting tube.

The air was a bit stale and smelled of grease and solvent, and he could hear a faint hiss of escaping air. *Must be a leak somewhere*, he thought uneasily. *Hope the whole place isn't like that. It sure wasn't the last time I was here, but that had to be three years ago.*

Wasn't it? The fact that he couldn't precisely remember bothered him. *Is this body going downhill already? Or is it normal to not remember details like that?* The uncertainty was nearly as bad as the memory loss.

"So, what do we do now?" Caree asked quietly.

"Looks like company is coming," Rake nodded toward an approaching man in a dirty brown uniform, flanked by two armed guards.

The station's staff made no pretense at friendliness. "Rake Weston. Different ship than the last time through."

"Not mine," Rake said as he jerked his thumb toward Caree. "Hers."

"Who's paying the fees?"

"Rake volunteered," Caree said casually.

He grunted a reluctant agreement. "From my account on file," he said. "We also need to fuel the ship."

"Fuel's hard to come by," the unarmed man said. "Expensive to get out here."

"Five," Rake said.

"Ha! Didn't know you were a comedian, Weston. Twelve."

"For twelve I could buy a ship with a full tank of fuel," he said with a shake of his head. "Seven, no more."

"Eight, and I send someone out to scrub the windows," the staffer said dryly.

"Fine, eight. How long?"

"It'll be slow," the station's negotiator said. "The passives we have on the ring shows a couple of Lantash sloops headed this way. They haven't found us yet, but we'll have to run the lines manually. No heavy equipment when the authorities are that close. Two hours, maybe?"

"Less would be more," Rake said.

"I'll see what we can do. In the meantime, are you going to enjoy our local facilities?"

"Just the pub. Which way?"

The man pointed down one of the shafts hewn from the stone of the rings. "Surprised you even have to ask. And I have to ask, what happened to your ship?" the man asked. "I've never seen another like it, and it'd be a shame if some authorities got their hands on it."

"Just on my way to retrieve her," Rake said casually. "No one flies my ship but me, and no one will ever catch her, either."

The negotiator and his two flunkies disappeared toward the docking ring and the *Starfall*, presumably to start the fueling process, while Rake led Caree down the stone hallway toward the pub. "You handled that well," the captain commented. "You've been here a few times, haven't you?"

Rake shrugged nonchalantly. "A couple times. It's a good refueling hole, and not a lot of people know about it. Those that do know keep their mouths shut, which is why there's a smuggler hole this close to a 'civilized' world." He raised an eyebrow at her. "Your crew *will* keep their mouths shut, won't they?"

"I'm insulted," Caree said, her tone sharp.

"Hey, secrecy keeps a *lot* of smugglers alive, including me. I don't want one of my holes compromised."

"You might have already compromised them by sending us here with those patrol boats chasing us," she retorted.

"Doubtful," he said dismissively. "They've kept their heads down plenty of times when the local authorities are orbiting overhead. Dozens of meters of solid rock is a good cover, as long as no one goes in or out with a sloop nearby. Now," he added as they stepped out of the passageway and into a larger, dimly-lit cavern, "let's just relax with a few drinks while they refuel the *Starfall*."

Like the passageways, the cavern had been carved from the solid stone of the rings. The ceilings were rather low - barely two and a half meters high - but the room itself was nearly sixty meters across, roughly circular. A handful of passageways led away from the pub, with dozens of small niches carved into the walls to provide privacy.

Lamps rose from the floor, a scant meter high, providing the sparse illumination. Power cables and cords were strung openly across the floor, trip hazards that the pub's proprietor didn't seem to care about. Tables, sparsely occupied, were scattered through the open space, some near lamps and some shrouded in darkness. There seemed to be little pattern to the lights and the tables, and the lack of order bothered Rake just a bit.

He didn't let his discomfort show as he led Caree toward the center of the pub.

The pub's owner and operator, a too-thin woman barely in her twenties but tougher than the stone walls of her business, was busy cleaning a sink full of plates, her back toward Rake and Caree. The bar cut a neat, illuminated circle in the middle of the pub, with a small cooking range and stove at the center of that.

"Rake Weston," she said gravely without turning her head. "What in the hell are you doing here?"

"Alo, Meg," he said easily as he slid onto one of the stools ringing the bar. "How's business?"

"Quiet. I like it that way." She turned away from her dishes, eyeing Rake warily. "Your poison?"

"Couple of your local brew," he ordered. "One for me, one for the captain."

Meg raised both eyebrows as she produced a pair of dark bottles from under the bar. With practiced ease she twisted both tops off simultaneously and set them down before the spacers. "Didn't know you would work for someone else."

"Not my preference, but I do what I have to do." He picked up the nearer brew and gestured for Caree to take the other. The captain gave him a dubious glance but took a drink, which was followed by a surprised look and a longer, slower pull.

Meg smiled at Caree. "Zero-gee brewing, Cap. Can't make a brew that'll touch mine if you're stuck on a planet."

The captain frowned. "But you have gravity here."

"Artificial, just like your ship," Meg explained. "And only in the habitable places. Storerooms are all packed tight with the grav shut off, unless there's some reason for it."

Rake took a swallow of the beer and smiled. "Nobody could brew like you, Meg, even if they *could* figure out your secrets."

"Such a flatterer, Rake." She raised a blonde eyebrow at him. "So, what are you doing working for someone else, and showing them this little hidey-hole?"

"On my way to Clarion to get my ship," Rake clarified. "This is a short-term gig only."

"I'd heard a rumor you got yourself killed on Clarion," Meg said dubiously. "You have to make a run for it without your ship?"

"Something like that," Rake smiled. "So what, exactly, have you heard?"

"Well, popular rumor was you took a job you shouldn't have - something for Boss Bruno. Whole thing went south, and you got killed by some of Bruno's lackeys on Clarion." She laughed as she twisted the top off a brew for herself, taking a long, slow pull. "'Course, that all seems rather foolish with you standing here."

"Mmmhmm," Rake said noncommittally as he took another swallow of beer. Fear soured the taste, though.

Oscar Bruno. What the hell was I thinking to take a job from him?

"What doesn't make sense about the whole thing," Meg continued, "is that there's still a price on your head. I checked the ComNet when I heard you were trying to land here with your old code. See, you landed here a few weeks ago with that code and picked up a new one. Between that, you being reported dead, and a price still on your head, tells me you had an insurance policy."

Rake set his beer down on the bar silently. He opened his mouth to respond, but found himself struggling for words when he saw a pistol in Meg's hand, leveled straight at his forehead.

VI

RAKE SHRUGGED AS HE PICKED up his beer, leaving his free hand on the bar, and took a long, slow pull.

Well, this couldn't get much worse, he decided.

"See, I can't believe you'd be so dumb as to walk in here with a price on your head," Meg continued. "Seriously, Weston. A hundred thousand bounty, and you come walking into my pub like you own the whole ring." She shook her head sadly. "Rake, you're a damned fool."

"Give me a break, Meg," he grumbled. "I've been getting shot at since I woke up at an insurance facility over Terra. I'm stumbling around trying to figure what I got into two weeks ago, and I've already got a skiptracer and the local patrols chasing me around. Now you're going to shoot me, too?"

The small woman snorted and laid the pistol down on the bar, picking up her beer instead. "Of course not. I just wanted to make my point."

"Consider it made." Rake studied his mostly-empty bottle as he turned it over in his head. "You said I was here?"

"A couple weeks ago, yeah. Said you were on a new job, a big score that could set you for quite a while." Meg drained her bottle in one long drink and tossed the bottle into a recycler behind the bar. "You didn't say what the job was, of course, except that it was big-time."

"What ship did I have when I came through?" Rake asked casually.

"You were flying that souped-up freighter of yours," Meg replied with a frown. "Why?"

"Just trying to put pieces together. Which way was I going at the time?"

"You didn't say - though you did mention you'd just come from Terra."

"That must have been right after you flashed your brain," Caree theorized.

"So I got the job sometime between leaving the insurance facility and arriving here," Rake mused. "If it came over the longcast, I'd have the recording in my radio system on the ship." He glanced over at Caree. "We need to get my ship back as soon as possible."

"Don't worry, I'll just tell Wings to make our next jump all the way across the Expanse," she said sarcastically. "I'm sure Joy can calculate that kind of a jump. I mean, it's not like the best navigation computers built can't do that."

"No need to get snippy with me," Rake grumbled.

"There is when your head's not on straight," Caree shot back. "Sarcasm is the only thing that can penetrate your skull when you quit listening with your ears."

"As entertaining as this all is," Meg said offhandedly, "maybe we can at least figure out where your next jump was."

"How?" Caree and Rake asked in unison.

"From here, you've got a few places you could've jumped, right?" Meg reasoned. "Back to Terra, for one. Most people heading out to the edge of the known worlds would head to Huaxa. Only other jump to take would be to Rika, but who would bother with that?"

Rake grunted his agreement. "Rika's a wreck after the Great War. That's what happens when you sit on one of the three routes that connects the two ends of the Expanse - even if it is the long way around."

"There's plenty of repopulation efforts going on there," Caree objected. "A cargo hold full of money to be had there."

"Right, but it'd all be legitimate contracts from Terra, right?" Meg asked. "Lots of official attention there - not a lot of room for whatever big score Rake was working on."

"So, more than likely on to Huaxa," Rake mused. "That would explain the mix-up with Boss Bruno. Every criminal pie up in that end of the Expanse has his thumb in it." He shook his head. "Not real useful, though. From

Huaxa there's a dozen worlds I could've been heading out to, assuming I wasn't taking the fastest route. Not useful at all."

Meg's face fell. "Sorry."

"There hasn't been any notices from local authorities for a reward for Rake, has there?" Caree asked.

The bartender shook her head. "Not a peep from the locals, and nothing from Terra, either."

"I didn't realize Boss Bruno had enough pull this close to Terra to get the local authorities chasing you, Rake," Caree noted uneasily. "Lantash is only one jump from Terra, and they don't abide our kind around here. Think he's buying up local politicians?"

"Doubtful," Rake said quietly. "Terra's navy hasn't recovered from the war, but if Bruno made a move that overt, the military would have to hunt him down. They can't allow anyone to encroach that far into their borders."

"So why are the locals chasing you, then?" Meg asked.

"When Slade was dragging me out of that insurance facility, he mentioned a Colonel Velles," Rake answered grimly. "I'd bet real money he's a higher-up in the Terra military. At first I thought he was bluffing, but now...well, whatever that job was, I pissed off both the law and the biggest criminal kingpin alike."

"A colonel is high-ranking on Terra?" Caree asked dubiously.

"Most of the flag officers were with Terra's fleet, just like the Earth Protection Navy." Rake finally finished his beer. "Given how both fleets just vanished, there weren't many officers or ships left. Terra's in no hurry to promote a bunch of officers to high ranks when there's no ships left to command." He nodded gratefully at Meg as she handed him another dark bottle. "If they have new warships coming out of the shipyards, the colonel could well be an admiral within a few years."

"I should leave you here," Caree grumbled. "Last thing I need is my ship plastered on Terran alert transmissions for the next five years."

"Thanks," he muttered.

A keening alarm sounded from under the bar. Meg frowned and crouched down, vanishing from sight for a moment. Her voice floated over the bar. "Alo."

"Meg, this is a general alert to all staff. We've had multiple warships jump in with Terra ident codes," the tinny voice said calmly. "They're all heading this way."

"Thanks," Meg said. She stood up from behind the bar, worry evident on her face. "Rake, you really know how to make friends, don't you?"

"We don't know they're looking for him," Caree objected. "It could just be a patrol."

"You really believe in coincidence?" Meg asked, her voice hard. "They just happen to be wandering by while there's two local sloops chasing you around? Even if Lantash is one of Terra's 'protectorates', that'd be a lot of bad luck."

"Okay, not likely," the captain allowed. "Still, they're not going to find this place. I've never seen a smuggler hole better hidden."

"You're right - they couldn't find it during the Great War, and they spent a lot of time looking for it back then," Meg agreed. "But if we keep this up, sooner or later they'll get lucky. And they only have to be lucky once."

"Guess we'll be sitting here until they give up," Rake grumbled. "That complicates things."

"Not complicates, just delays," Caree said. "Let's just have another drink, shall we? I'm sure we can find some way to occupy our time after that."

* * *

Fourteen hours later, the hangover had mostly abated. *Shouldn't have been a hangover at all*, Rake thought wearily. *I didn't drink that much. Is that one more sign this body is failing? I can't hold my liquor?*

He swallowed hard at the thought. *If I'm falling apart at the seams, I don't have a lot of time to figure this out. I need to figure out what this job was, collect the payoff, and get myself a new body grown before I die.*

"Good morning, handsome," Caree said drowsily as she entered the steam shower. "Sleep well?"

Rake pushed aside his fears about his failing body. "Very."

"Good. I'm glad that all our work last night was not a waste." She slapped his butt playfully. "Now, you look all clean, and I'd hate to change that, so you'd best go get dressed."

Rake shook his head. "Sure," he said. "Captain."

Caree laughed. "You could go find us a few more bottles of that brew," she suggested. "And see if our friends, the Terrans, have gotten any closer."

The pilot shrugged. "Sounds far more boring than staying here," he replied with a wink.

She laughed and pushed him out of the shower. "No wonder you've never signed onto anyone's crew. You can't follow an order to save your life!"

"So now you want to start giving me orders?" he asked. "That could be fun."

A towel smacked him in the face, and the door swung shut. He grinned as he wiped himself off, pulled on his clothes, and brushed his hair down with his hand. Suitably disheveled and with his borrowed pistol back at his hip, Rake headed out the *Starfall*'s airlock and back into the smuggler hole.

The *Starfall* had long since finished refueling, and the lines had been pulled away and securely stored. No other vessels had docked or left since the *Starfall*'s arrival, presumably due to the Terran fleet now hunting for them.

The walk back to the pub took longer than it had the previous day, mostly because Rake slowed every time he approached an overhead light. His head pounded as he walked, and he concluded he was more hungover than he had cared to admit in the shower.

Meg was at her usual place in the pub when he arrived, but unlike before, the cavernous bar was filled to standing-room only. The crowd was fairly loud as he approached, but when he stepped into the pub the entire crowd, several hundred strong, fell silent and turned to stare at him.

All eyes seemed to be locked on Rake as he picked his way through the crowd to the bar in the center of the room. Nonchalantly, he sat himself down on one of the stools and looked Meg square in the eyes. "One of your darks," he ordered in the silence.

Silently she twisted the lid off one of the bottles and set it down on the bar. He picked it up and took a long pull. "So, what news from the Terrans?" he asked conversationally.

"You haven't heard?" Meg half-whispered.

"I've been, uh, busy," he said.

"They offered a quarter-million for your head," she explained slowly. "They broadcast it locally. We've been trying to decide whether to turn you in."

"What's this 'we'?" he asked, a little offended.

Meg nodded at the crowd surrounding them. "We," she repeated.

"Ah." Rake took a long drink from the bottle, but the beer tasted sour from fear. "Don't mind me," he said loudly. "I'm just going to enjoy my drink while you decide whether to throw me out the airlock." He dropped his voice to ask Meg, "How long?"

"Six hours," she answered simply. "They took up orbit almost twelve hours ago, and apparently took their time making the demands."

"Did they give a timeline?" he asked.

"Not in so many words, no. But they've got thirty warships scattered around the orbit with guns pointed at the ring. I'm guessing they want an answer sooner, rather than later."

Rake raised both eyebrows at that. "Thirty warships?" he repeated.

"Most of them small," Meg expounded. "The two Lantash sloops have a half-dozen Terran friends, and half of the rest of the ships are corvettes. A handful of frigates, two cruisers, and one carrier."

"A carrier, huh? So do they have fighters out scouring the ring?" Rake asked.

She shook her head. "Not one of the sensor satellites have picked up a single fighter. They must be keeping them in reserve."

"In reserve?" Rake was skeptical. "There's no strategic reason I can think of to keep the fighters in reserve. That would be their best bet of intercepting the *Starfall* if we tried to run for it, but keeping them on the carrier means there's a very good chance they'll be out of position. No, they have to be up to something else."

"They're probably expecting us to give you up," Meg said. "If we did, then it doesn't matter whether the fighters are flying."

The loudspeakers strung throughout the entire facility crackled with life. "Incoming shortcast from the Terran fleet," a voice announced. "Patching through now."

"—have been given an adequate opportunity to turn over the criminal, Rake Weston," a new voice blared from the speaker, speaking in the official, clipped tones of a military officer. "Given your reluctance to comply, we will now commence operations. We continue until the criminal has been surrendered to us." The voice cut off as suddenly as it had begun.

"So, now what?" Rake mumbled. He stared down at his beer bottle, sitting utterly still on the countertop.

Ripples appeared in his beer, then vanished.

Rake frowned and squinted his eyes at the bottle.

The liquid trembled again, just for a few seconds, then stilled again.

"What the hell?" he muttered.

Voices began to rise in the pub. Rake ignored them, studying his beer. *Nobody's been moving. What's going on?*

Ripples again, this time more intensive. They seemed to last longer before vanishing.

Vibrations. Where are the vibrations coming from? He looked up at Meg, who wore a puzzled expression. "What is it, Rake?"

"Not sure," he muttered as he studied the bottle. The ripples came again, and again, the time between them shortening. The very next time, he swore he could feel the vibrations in his boots.

Meg caught his attention, fear in her eyes. "What's happening?" she hissed to him as the noise level in the pub reached a normal level.

"I don't..." He didn't have time to answer before the entire room rocked, glasses and bottles tipping and falling, sending spirits sloshing over tables and clothes, glass shattering on the hard stone floor.

Rake's bottle hadn't hit the floor before he was reaching across the bar and grabbing Meg's arm. "We have to get out of here!" he shouted.

"What's happening?" she hollered back over the sudden cacophony of shouts of surprise, shattering glass, and a low rumble that seemed to pervade everything.

"Come on!" he urged her, half-pulling her over the bar before she yielded to his order and started to scramble across herself. As she tried to slide to her feet, Rake reached over the counter and snagged a crate of Meg's dark bottles. *If I'm right, I'm going to need these to sweet-talk Caree when this is all over.*

As he half-dragged Meg toward the door, she kept hollering, "Rake, what's going on?!"

"They're bombing the ring!"

VII

THE PASSAGEWAYS WERE CROWDED WITH screaming people.

I would have thought a bunch of criminals would be more collected than this, he thought. As he pulled Meg through the crowd, he was sickened to realize why. *These aren't all criminals. This might be a smuggler hole, but most of the crew are just average people doing a job. I bet most of them have never been under the guns of a local patrol cruiser or* really *been in trouble. Most of these people have never even been* shot. *Now we've got nukes coming down on us.*

Rake and Meg had nearly reached the end of the tunnel when the roof gave way. Artificial gravity pulled the stone down, catching three unlucky souls right in front of Rake. Blood and dust rose in a red-tinted haze, and the smell alone brought horrid memories flooding back from the deep recesses of his mind he tried to ignore. Meg retched, and then the contents of her stomach were suddenly added to the stench already assaulting Rake's nose.

"Go back!" he shouted as he turned. "We need another way to the docking ring!"

Meg's face was green but her eyes determined. *She's a survivor*, Rake thought as she led him back down the tunnel.

The crowded tunnel was already reversing direction, but it was so tightly-packed that neither Meg nor Rake could force their way through. In spite of the eminent death awaiting both of them, Rake was grateful momentarily for the Terran ships orbiting nearby.

I got lucky one of their first strikes was near the base, he realized. *Everyone's so busy trying to save their own skins that they're not trying to turn me in. This has to be the worst good-luck any soul has ever had.*

They were the last people out of the tunnel emptying back into the pub. Meg didn't hesitate to pull Rake into another passageway, this one twisting "upward" relative to the pub. Rake's sense of direction screamed that she was leading him away from the *Starfall*, but he didn't allow himself to doubt.

She's your best chance for getting out of this alive. Stay with her unless she betrays you.

The tunnel abruptly ended, opening into another cavernous opening nearly as large as Meg's pub. This chamber, however, was furnished with electronics and computer consoles of all sorts. Meg slowed as they entered, then stopped entirely a half-dozen paces inside.

"Rake Weston," a man in a military-cut black suit called as he stepped forward, though there were no insignias of any sort pinned to his uniform. "Just to let you know, should we survive this, I don't think you'll be welcome back here."

"I can imagine not," Rake drawled. "What's going on?"

"Terrans have opened up with a patterned bombardment of tactical nuclear warheads," the man answered. "In the first three minutes of bombardment, there was a strike within twenty kilometers of here. It's shaken a lot of things apart."

"Wonderful," Rake muttered. "Have you extrapolated the pattern?"

The man nodded. "We'll have another strike here within ten minutes, and it's going to be just about right on our heads."

"How much of the ring are they bombarding?" Rake asked.

"The entire thing."

"They're bombing the *entire ring?*" Meg asked in disbelief. "All the way around the planet?"

"Yes," the man confirmed. "That's why they brought in so many warships, I'd guess. You could never do it effectively with two sloops, but with thirty warships? Yes, it'll still take time, but not nearly as long."

"Great," Rake muttered.

"We need to get out of here," Meg said. "What's open for passageways back to the *Starfall?*"

"Looks like the main cargo line is all that's left," the man said as he turned back to one of the displays splashed across glass. "Everything else will need to be cleared, assuming there's anything left when the Terrans quit dropping bombs on our heads."

"Great," Meg muttered. "And we have ten minutes to get there?"

"Nine, now," the man said dryly. "Good luck getting out of here. Everyone's scrambling to evac ships. We're ordering them all to hold position, but as soon as someone jumps out from cover we're going to have the whole Terran fleet shooting at us."

"At least this explains why they weren't using the fighters to search for us," Rake commented. "They didn't want them caught in the crossfire when they started raining hell down on us." He turned to Meg, pulled her around until he was looking squarely in her eyes. "Can you get us to the *Starfall*?"

She nodded.

"Then lead on."

* * *

Whether it was because most of the ring's population had already reached their ships, or because no one wanted to travel through the cargo shaft, Rake and Meg had little trouble reaching their destination. It was only when Meg explained what the next few minutes would entail that Rake realized *why* no one else was trying the cargo shaft.

Very few people liked navigating a gravity-less environment while encumbered with an air suit.

In hindsight, it made sense, of course - it took far less power to leave the gigantic shaft without gravity or air, given that most of the equipment was handled by AIs. It also made cargo easier to move, and eliminated the need for heavier machinery that would require additional maintenance.

"Really? Your idea is to throw ourselves out the airlock and *float* to the other end?" Rake asked dubiously as he reluctantly suited up for the zero-gee vacuum that awaited.

"Not throw - more like violently decompress the airlock to get us momentum," Meg corrected.

"Will that work?"

"Maybe you'd rather go back and wait for the next missile to hit?" she asked sarcastically.

"Alright, then."

Rake waited impatiently while Meg fiddled with an override panel. The airlock controls weren't a style he was familiar with, and he resisted the urge to push her aside and handle it himself. *It'll probably take you longer than it will her if you just leave her alone. Patience.*

And abruptly, the outer airlock door slammed open.

Given the inner door was still open, Rake hadn't expected it. The air seemed to boil around them and into the void, shoving him off his feet and into oblivion.

Fear held him tightly as he thrashed around, his efforts entirely worthless with no gravity and nothing within reach. He helplessly floated along as the air flooding into the cargo shaft carried him.

It was only belatedly that he realized Meg was a half-dozen meters away. He keyed the air suit's radio. "Thanks for the warning."

"Get ready to jump," she said cheerfully.

"Aren't you worried about all the air emptying into here?" he asked tightly. "I mean, you kind of left the airlock open."

"When the command center gets an alert about a drop in air pressure, which should be any minute now, they'll force the airlock doors to close," she explained. "Until then, this works way better than the little boost we'd have gotten if I'd closed the interior door first and just used the air in the lock."

Rake had to agree as he studied the unlit cut stone shaft, just barely able to see enough detail to get a sense of their speed. *We're probably moving thirty klicks an hour*, he realized.

"How long is this shaft?" he asked Meg.

"About a klick and a half."

"So how long until we reach the other end?"

"Oh, about now."

Rake twisted around to look "up" in the darkness in time to see a darkened steel door.

The man barely had time to react, to protect his head, when he smashed into the airlock. He had been tumbling in the air and landed almost squarely on his chest, knocking the breath from his lungs and sending him into a dizzying spin. Meg, far more in control, caught his flailing hand as she snagged a safety bar mounted beside the outer door.

Rake hung limply in Meg's grasp as he tried to straighten out his spinning head. "I should have left you behind," he complained.

"You would never have gotten this far without me," she replied cheerfully. A moment later, the door hissed open and she swung him through, then followed with a fluid jump of her own. Artificial gravity caught them both, and Rake added several more new bruises to his already extensive collection as he bounced along the floor.

Meg landed far more gracefully, a controlled tumble that ended with her on top of Rake. "Thanks for breaking my fall," she added.

"I'm just glad the floor broke mine," he muttered.

"Come on, we're almost out of time," Meg urged him as she keyed the outer door shut and the inner door open. Air rushed in, nearly bowling over the rising Rake.

They shed bits of the awkward air suits as they ran, leaving the discarded pieces behind like refuse. From the airlock, it was only a few hundred meters to the *Starfall*, and Rake was kicking off the last of his suit, the boots, as he reached the boarding ramp.

Caree was standing at the foot of the ramp, arms crossed and clearly unhappy. "Rake, didn't I tell you to go get some of that dark and not cause any problems?" she hollered over the ominous rumbling as another salvo of missiles struck none-too-distantly.

"Sorry, I dropped the dark somewhere along the way," he confessed.

"What's going on?" she asked.

"Terran navy decided to nuke the entire ring," Rake said grimly as he climbed the ramp with Meg beside him. "Everyone here is standing by to evac when the command center gives the order."

Caree eyed him warily. "Are you thinking what I think you're thinking?"

Rake shrugged uneasily. "We *did* bring this down on them."

"Not *we*. *You* did."

He nodded. "Yes, I did."

"Then it's time to haul ass out of here."

* * *

The bridge of the *Starfall* was fully occupied when Rake stepped through the hatch, but that didn't stop him from walking straight to the pilot's chair. "You're sitting in my chair," he announced coolly.

Wings looked up at him, then looked past him to Caree. She nodded in affirmation. Silently, the pilot unstrapped and stood up. Rake hardly let him step away before he was sliding in and strapping into the chair.

The *Starfall* wasn't his ship, so he spent a few moments familiarizing himself with the controls. Not unlike his own vessel, the *Starfall*'s primary control was a pilot's yoke, studded with buttons and switches to give him precision access to the engines and maneuvering thrusters - access he'd need for what he was about to attempt. Displays seemed to wrap around him, showing everything from relative altitude, acceleration, and speed to fuel levels to system temperatures to local geography.

The navigator, Joy, would feed him critical information on the geography display, but ultimately, Rake had control.

"Are we flight ready?" he called tightly.

"Reactor, engines, weapons, sensors, navigation, computers, all green-lighted and ready," Caree professionally reported.

"Good. Get us a jump to Terra plotted," Rake said as he tested the play of his controls, trying to get a good feel for their limits of motion.

"Terra? With the Terran navy breathing down our necks?" Caree asked in surprise.

"The alternative is Huaxa, and a long, long way around to Clarion. Besides, with most of the Terran navy here, there won't be much for patrols *there*. We can skip right through the other side and jump to Spiri."

She nodded at Joy. "Plot the course."

Rake studied his displays one more time. "Looks like they're setting up for the next strike," he said grimly. "As soon as it hits, we're gone."

"I thought we were waiting for the order to go," Meg protested as Rake's hand settled on the throttle.

"We brought this down on you," Caree said. "We're going to take it away."

"If you blow cover now, you'll reveal exactly where the base is," Meg tried.

"We're not going to blow cover now. We're going to blow cover when that missile hits," Rake explained confidently. "And here it comes."

He settled in, watching the displays uneasily. Long experience had taught him not to trust what computers told him; electronic counter measures were effective tools during the Great War. Veterans had learned to only depend on what they could see with their own two eyes; anything else could be a computerized mistake.

Thus Rake fretted while he watched the nuclear warhead descend toward the ring, unable to visually see it, but clearly drawn out on a sensor board. He gripped the controls tightly, one hand on the throttle array, the other on the yoke.

Then the missile hit.

Rake was already feeding power to the engines in anticipation, and the *Starfall* groaned under the sudden stress as he slammed power to the thrusters. The vessel squirted out from under the stone outcropping just as the warhead detonated above.

He was hauling back on the yoke, pulling the *Starfall*'s nose up, when rock shaken loose by the nearby strike began to rain down into the canyon. Rake's eyes were as wide as saucers as he slammed the throttle forward and jerked the yoke back harder, barely avoiding a boulder that would have crushed the ship flat.

More stones were breaking free from the concussion, swirling in all directions in the low-gee environment. He tried to look everywhere as he poured more power to the engines, slipping back and forth to avoid showers of stone that would cripple the ship.

And then they were above the canyon. The rugged terrain of the ring spread out in all directions, seemingly flat. Rake immediately leveled off and firewalled the throttle.

The abrupt acceleration shoved everyone back in their seats, hard, but Rake reveled in the sensation. *This* was flying - it had felt so wrong before, forced to sit in a jump seat and watch while someone else, some lesser pilot, took control of the ship and put it through its paces. The vibrations, the noises, the sensations that had bothered him before were now streams of data providing the critical input he needed to fly.

"ECM is cranked up," Joy reported from the navigation station. "ECCM is commencing from the warships."

"How much can you do?" Rake asked calmly between gritted teeth.

"I can keep their missiles from lighting us up and mess with their anticipatory targeting for the coilguns, but we're as bright as a star on their sensors."

"That'll do," Rake managed. "What's the fleet doing?"

"They're not reacting yet - I think we caught them with their pants down."

Rake merely grunted an acknowledgement as he kept the freighter accelerating along the ring. He was low enough that mountain peaks thrust up like grasping fingers around them, but high enough to give himself time to anticipate. Still, as their velocity mounted, he knew he'd be forced to leave cover soon - their continual acceleration would leave the *Starfall* too sluggish to adequately maneuver to avoid the obstacles in her way.

"More detonations, directly ahead!" Joy shouted.

Stone seemed to rise directly toward them, and Rake was forced to make a decision. *Break for open space, or try to draw their fire?* The best thing for the *Starfall's* survival, of course, would be to break for open space and get far enough away from major gravity fields to make their jump to Terra. However, the longer they surfed the debris floating up from the bombardment, the better the odds of drawing more Terran warships to them, giving the occupants of the smuggler base time to evacuate.

Rake pulled the throttle back, cutting the engines to a minimum. In orbit, their momentum would carry them along at the speeds they'd already reached, or near enough. He pushed the yoke forward and dove toward the rising stone.

Then the *Starfall* was in the deadly shower. Sweat poured down Rake's forehead and stung his eyes as he maneuvered wildly through the free-floating rocks with no goal but survival. Joy madly fed him data on the masses of stone, offering him velocities, courses, likely collisions, but it was too tumultuous for the *Starfall*'s computers to offer him more than a best guess.

"Warships are breaking off bombardment and moving toward our position," Caree said tersely. "I think it's time to get out of here, Rake."

"Fun's just getting started," he said tightly as another shard of rock flashed by so closely he could see scratches in its sheared surface.

"More fun than you think," the captain retorted. "That carrier's launched fighters, and they're vectoring on us."

"Okay, maybe it *is* time to get out of here," Rake said with a wild grin. He punched the throttle again as he pulled back on the yoke, and then the *Starfall* was climbing away from the meteor storm. The rocks fell back in their wake, unable to do any further harm.

Except one.

The screech of torn metal sent a shiver through Rake's teeth, and he winced at the pain. Red lights flashed on his status boards, but he ignored them, as he would any machine that told him, *No, you can't do it.* The engines roared too loudly as he held the yoke steady, guiding the vessel out into space.

The Terran fleet had broken their orbital positions to pursue, but even at their maximum acceleration they couldn't catch the fleeing freighter. Some of the capital ships tried to reach out with coilguns, firing projectiles along best-guess trajectories to try to catch their prey. It was to no avail, however, as the *Starfall* gently changed course every few seconds, just enough to throw off the computer-assisted aim of the Terran gunners.

But there was one thing that could catch them: the fighters.

The concept of starfighters had been initially laughed out of meetings by the war planners.

Why build such small and limited craft? There is no purpose for vessels with such short range and no point drives. Computer-targeted anti-air cannons will tear them to shreds before they can reach an effective range. No, guided missiles will be a far more effective use of resources.

It wasn't until the second year of the Great War that a Terran admiral, frustrated by long-range, inaccurate duels with Earth's fleet and sophisticated ECM leading to inconclusive engagements, had insisted on trialing a number of small craft. The initial starfighters had been mere missiles with most of their computerized guidance systems ripped out and life-support systems installed, all around a tiny cockpit. The war planners smugly deemed the little craft useless - after all, a missile with a man could not accelerate like its unmanned counterparts without killing the pilot, and would certainly be taken to pieces by the automated defense guns of the Earth fleets.

The laughter had died when the tiny "manned missiles" using small, lightweight ECM had slipped through the defenses of an entire Earth-Loyalist fleet and crippled the engines of six warships using nothing but small-bore coilguns, finally withdrawing only after expending their ammunition stores.

Locked on their courses by the cruelty of Sir Isaac Newton, the vessels were picked apart by a Terran fleet far out of the usual combat range. No ECM could counter the simple math of a ship with no engines stuck on a trajectory in open space.

The Terrans had stuck with simple starfighter designs throughout the war, usually deploying them in the same way: slip through the enemy's ECM and inflict damage on a ship, leaving it vulnerable to the distant heavy-hitters of the Terran navy. It had been a simple, devastating technique that served the Terrans well through the end of the war.

And now, those simple starfighters - not much larger than the nuclear-armed warheads that had been fired into the rings - were quickly closing the gap.

"Do we still have guns?" Rake asked as he calculated the numbers.

"Yes," Caree said after a moment, "but they're not going to be good against anything that small or fast."

"Set them in our wake and start bursting fire. If we make the fighters evade at all, we'll be ready to jump before they can catch us."

Caree smiled as she keyed commands into her console. "Done."

Rake glanced at his screens. The fighters were a minute back - far enough that their sensors were unlikely to pick up the *Starfall*'s coilguns firing. Sure enough, as he watched, one of the fighters was unlucky enough to catch a few shots, and its intercept course suddenly became a tumbling mess as the fighter was thrown off by the impact, the engines pushing the tiny ship in all directions.

The flight commander was no idiot - the fighters began to evade, juking enough to ensure nothing short of an extremely unlucky shot would strike, but their rate of closure slowed.

"Jump laid in," Joy announced. "We're ready."

"Engaging point drive," Caree stated. A moment later, space twisted all around them, and Lantash was light-years away.

VIII

NTERESTING WORLD, CLARION," CAREE COMMENTED as she studied the blue-white globe rotating on the *Starfall*'s largest display. "If it wouldn't have been for the war, this place would have a population to rival Terra."

Rake couldn't disagree as he watched the image. The planet was well outside the most heavily populated worlds, and had been discovered less than thirty years ago. The planet had been cleared for human habitation less than three years before the Great War broke out, and barely a million settlers had started setting up cities before all funding was diverted to the war effort.

"Eighty-five percent of the surface is water," Wings commented. "With the land largely broke up in chunks smaller than a hundred thousand square klicks. Anywhere you want me to set us down, we'll have tropical breezes and beaches."

Caree just shook her head. "Almost no axial tilt, all that water, right square in the temperate zone. This planet was practically created to be a tropical paradise. Mark my words, someday this place will be the biggest tourist trap in the Expanse."

"As long as that day isn't today," Rake spoke up. "We're just lucky that doubling back to Terra threw off that fleet. You'll need to lay low for a while, probably get your identification codes changed, maybe even overhaul the engine so it doesn't throw the same energy patterns - anything to make sure the *Starfall* doesn't get tagged the next time you hit a civilized system."

"What, you're not coming with us?" Caree asked.

Rake shook his head. "I was pretty sure you wanted me off your ship. I've brought you plenty of trouble already."

The woman gave him a smile hot enough to melt through hull armor. "Not just trouble."

The pilot snickered. "Besides, I can't afford to keep traveling with you. My credit account won't hold out."

Caree exchanged glances with her crew. "We're in this for the money, Weston. With Boss Bruno and the Terrans all after you, there has to be some profit in this somewhere - besides turning you over, of course," she added with a wink. "So you're stuck with us for now."

Rake managed to hide a smile. "Or at least until my account is zeroed out. So, what's your plan?"

"We don't usually operate in this part of the Expanse," Caree admitted. "Do you have a recommendation on a shop? Some place to get our repairs done?"

"Yeah, actually," he answered. He stepped over to Caree's command chair and watched as the image of Clarion rotated, finally jabbing a finger on an island in the northern hemisphere. "There."

"That seems rather vague," Caree said dryly.

"The place is called the 'Wirst Shop'," Rake explained. "Best starship mechanic I've ever dealt with, without a doubt. He can handle a quick engine overhaul and have you setup with new ID codes in a couple of days."

"You really want us to go to a place called the Worst Shop?" Joy asked skeptically.

"Wirst, not worst," he corrected. "It's his middle name."

"What's his last name, 'Mechanic'?" Wings joked.

Rake shook his head. "Laugh all you want, but he's the best chance you've got to get all the work done in a quick way."

"And what about your ship?" Caree asked with a raised eyebrow. "Where are we going to pick it up, and are we really going to fly both our freighters back out of here?"

The pilot could only shrug helplessly. "I've got a pretty good idea that the ship is here - I'll just have to figure out where I left it."

Caree nodded at Wings. "Start our descent. I'd assume there's no real traffic control to worry about, so get us in the area and then light up the radio until we find this Wirst Shop." She looked up at Rake and gestured for him to lean in before whispering, "I haven't heard anything from that barkeep you dragged with us, and no one's seen her out of her room. Do you want to check on her?"

Rake nodded and headed aft without further word.

Warships tended to bury their command centers deep inside the hull to protect from hostile weapons fire and free-floating debris. Crew quarters were squeezed in where possible, often just forward of the bridge, or even packed around it.

By contrast, noncombat vessels preferred to have the bridge either at the nose of the ship or at the very top to allow the pilot and officers to visually look around at their surroundings. The rest of the forward hull was usually filled with cargo space, to allow goods to be moved in and out easily whether the ship was sitting on the ground or merely connected with another space-going craft via airlocks. In the aft of the ship would be the necessary equipment for a ship - engines, computers, life support equipment, and crew amenities, including galleys, waste disposal, and bunks.

The *Starfall*'s crew quarters were just forward of the main engine; the passage leading back to the engine was actually lined with doors leading to sleeping chambers. In the case of the *Starfall*, they had dedicated the rooms closer to the engine for the crew, while the chambers further forward were used by guests.

Rake stopped at the very first doorway and tapped. "Meg?" he asked quietly. "Meg, are you there?"

When there was no answer, he tried the latch and found it unlocked. He tapped the release, but the door didn't move. *Wonderful - the door sliders are broken.* Rake leaned in and pulled the door with a powerful jerk.

Slowly, the portal slid open to reveal darkened quarters. *This is the right room, isn't it?* Rake wondered.

Then he heard the quiet sniffling.

"Meg?" he asked softly.

"What do you want, Rake?" the thin voice asked from a corner.

He squinted and peered through the gloom, and was finally able to make out a dim shape curled up on the end of a cot, tightly snuggled into the corner of the room. "Thought I'd come check on you. Have you eaten anything since we left Lantash?"

"No," she said, her voice so faint he had to strain to hear it over the slowly-increasing roar of the engine as the *Starfall* began to descend into Clarion's atmosphere. "Why?"

"Because you need to eat, just like the rest of us," Rake said.

"Why bother?" Meg asked, her voice thready.

"You lost your bar, but the universe is going to keep on spinning," Rake answered quietly but firmly. "You need to keep spinning, too. Nothing's going to stop and wait for you."

"Rake, what happened at Lantash...did anyone else even survive?" she asked, her voice barely audible.

"I don't know," he replied honestly. "We have no way of knowing. When we broke cover and made our flashy exit, the Terran navy took off to chase us. The smuggler hole took a lot of damage, but they're probably alright. Hell, maybe your bar is still there and you can go back."

"Go back?" she said, the first note of hope entering her voice.

"It's possible," Rake reaffirmed with a nod. "I'm sure they'd like their pub back in working order. Besides, I've been to every world in the Expanse, and I've never tasted a dark better than yours."

"So where are we?" Meg asked, sniffling a bit.

"Clarion. Tropical paradise world."

"Tropical paradise?" she asked with a disbelieving half-sob, half-snort. "You're joking, right? Everyone knows worlds aren't the same all over."

"Nope, I'm not joking. It just had the misfortune of not being fully settled when the war broke out," Rake said. "Besides, when was the last time you were off the Ring?"

"When I was six years old," Meg said.

Rake couldn't help but stare. "You've been living there for fifteen years?" he asked.

"Eleven," Meg corrected. "After Dad disappeared, I had nowhere to go and no reason to leave, or even a *way* to leave."

Rake shook his head. *She hasn't seen an open sky in years and years. Wonder how she'll take it?* "You probably want to find something cool to wear," he told her. "It's going to be hot and humid when we land, and you'll be a lot more comfortable that way."

"What about me?" Meg asked.

Rake gave her a quizzical look.

"Are you just going to leave me here?" she asked quietly. "I already know I won't do anything but slow you down."

The pilot had to stop and consider that.

She's right, of course. She's not going to be helpful in tracking down what happened in the last two weeks, especially given she's got no experience off the Ring. She's old enough to look out for herself, too; she doesn't need another father. The logic was clean and cool, but Rake didn't feel real comfortable with the direction it took him. *Of course, it's your fault her pub was reduced to a pile of rubble, and you've dragged her halfway across the Expanse to a world where she has no friends or allies, and definitely no one to look out for her.*

"I'll make a deal with you," Rake told her seriously.

"What are the terms?" she asked, an edge of defensiveness in her voice.

She was living by herself on the Ring for years, running a pub. She's probably got no trust for spacers - likely a good number of them wanted one thing from her, and one thing only.

"You stick with Caree and the *Starfall* and get yourself some time on Clarion relaxing and thinking about what you want to do next," Rake said, "and we'll talk before I leave. If you want to go with me, you can; if you've got a different direction you want to go, you're on your own. Okay?"

"Okay," she said, wiping her eyes before rising from the cot and offering her hand. "It's a deal."

As he shook Meg's hand, Rake couldn't help but think that her grip was the envy of spacers far older and stronger than she. "Deal."

* * *

The *Starfall*'s engine was deafening when Rake left Meg's quarters and headed back toward the bridge. Between the noise and the steadily-increasing vibration throughout the deck, Rake guessed they were within a few minutes of landing. *Sooner I can get out of here and find my ship, the better*, he told himself. *Hopefully Wirst can help me out.*

By the time he reached the *Starfall*'s bridge, the vibrations were falling off as the ship leveled out. The vessel had perhaps two thousand meters of altitude left; the oceans were clearly visible through the viewports, with a scattering of islands visible below.

"Ah, good timing, Rake," Caree said as he stepped into the command room. "We've found the Wirst Shop, but they're asking for a landing code."

Rake paused for a moment before rattling off a series of letters and numbers. Joy, handling the radio from her navigational station, repeated the passcode without hesitating. A moment later, she nodded and offered a small smile. "We have a landing beacon."

"Take us in, Wings," Caree ordered. She glanced at Rake questioningly, but he merely shook his head as he tried to quell his unease.

* * *

Rake's unease deepened as he led the *Starfall*'s crew, plus Meg, down the boarding ramp. Wirst himself stood at the foot of the ramp with his arms crossed, four of his mechanics standing in loose semicircle behind him. That wouldn't have been unusual in and of itself, but all four of the men were armed with carbines.

This isn't Wirst's style at all, Rake thought in dismay.

"Weston," the chief grunted when they were only a few meters apart.

"Wirst. What's going on? Am I not welcome around here anymore?" Rake asked.

Well, that came out worse than I thought it would. Oops.

"Well, I haven't rightly decided," Wirst drawled, lifting his cap off before scratching the top of his head. "What kind of trouble have you gotten yourself into, and when did you start flying on someone else's ship?"

Rake considered carefully before he answered, but finally chose to ignore the logical voice whispering to play it close to his chest. "Well, I got killed somewhere out here. I needed a ride back to recover my ship. Don't suppose you know where I parked it, do you?"

Wirst's eyes widened. "You fool kid, what did you get yourself into? I knew it was something when a few of Bruno's thugs started poking around, but I figured you owed some money - nothing you'd get killed over."

"That's what I've been trying to figure out," Rake said dryly. "Since I woke up in an insurance facility over Terra,

I've had skiptracers and Terran military all trying to nail me. I've barely been able to stop and breathe, let alone find out what I did."

Wirst was shaking his head the entire time. "So, I take it this ship has been tagged?" he asked.

Caree stepped forward. "We're pretty certain both our engine signature and our ID codes are plastered all over the Terran military network," she answered. "I was hoping you could help us out."

Wirst glanced up at the ship, seeming to take it all in with a single look. "We'll need to get it under cover and start stripping down the engine right away," he said authoritatively. "We'll have a new ident code package programmed in within an hour, but the engine signature will take longer."

He waved to the armed mechanics, and they immediately scattered into the outlying buildings. In less than a minute, they were returning with the heavy equipment necessary to roll the starship inside the largest hangar, which stood nearly eighty meters high.

"You all," Wirst said, addressing the *Starfall*'s crew, "feel free to use the house down closest to the water. It's empty right now, and there should be plenty of food to go around. You look like you could use some relaxation."

"Thank you, yes," Caree said. "What will we owe you?"

"Don't worry," Wirst said with a wink, "I'll charge it to Weston's account."

Rake could only grimace, and he held the expression until the *Starfall*'s crew had all started walking toward the beach house. Then he turned to Wirst and raised both eyebrows. "So, when did Bruno's thugs leave?" he asked tightly.

"Not six hours before you dropped in here," Wirst said grimly. "How'd you know?"

"You asked for the security code from a ship that'd never been here. If everything were normal, you'd have had us set down at an outlying pad until you figured out who we were and if we could be trusted." Rake frowned at the wizened old man. "You didn't bring much firepower, though. If we had come out with guns blazing we could've walked right over your men."

The master mechanic snorted. "I had six men with longcoils holed up in the hangar, back in the dark where you couldn't see them. If you had so much as touched that ugly pistol on your hip, they would've added a couple of holes to your mug."

Wirst led Rake away from the slowly-moving *Starfall*, apparently feeling no need to oversee the operation. "So, got yourself killed, did you?"

"Clearly," Rake said dryly. "When did I come through here?"

"Three or four days ago, and you were still flying your ship," Wirst answered. "When you left here, you were at the helm."

"What did I need?" the pilot asked.

The older man snorted. "You wanted your navigational record wiped clean," he said.

"My nav record?" Rake repeated in disbelief, trying to assimilate the new information.

"Yes, your nav record," Wirst said. "Geeze, kid, did they put you in a bad body? Can't hear what I'm saying? Yes, you asked me to wipe your nav record for anything older than your trip from Earth to Clarion. You'd managed to wipe out your record for your last jump before that, but you were afraid someone might be able to put it back together."

"What do you remember from my nav data?" Rake asked.

Wirst shook his head. "I didn't pry, boy - I just did what you asked."

The pilot closed his eyes as he mulled it over. "So, I was trying to cover my tracks - and the trail picked up at Earth. There's, what, six jumps I could've been making from there?" he mused. "And that would just be a single jump. I could've gone a lot of different directions."

"Not really your style to travel that side of the Expanse, either," Wirst commented. "You usually stay on the Terra side of things."

"That's because Terra and Viapori are the homes of what's left of the Terran navy, and Rika is a graveyard," Rake said. "My options are to wave at all those nice, heavily armed, law-abiding ships, or go tripping through a system that has more corpses than Earth." He shuddered in distaste. "No, thank you."

"But something apparently sent you out that way," Wirst pointed out. "You had to go through one of those places if you were at Earth."

It wasn't a pleasant thought.

"Did I say anything else while I was here?" Rake asked. "Something that would have given you an idea what I was involved in, or any clue about who I was working for?"

"Boss Bruno's thugs were the only thing that told me who you were working for," Wirst retorted. "You know my policy, Weston - I don't ask questions, and I don't want more information than I need to do my job. It's better for everyone that way."

"So there's nothing." Rake deflated as he thought it over.

Of course I didn't tell him anything. I play everything too close to my chest. In this case, that means I have no way of knowing where I went or what I was working on. Wonderful. Absolutely wonderful. He swallowed, but his own saliva seemed to stick in his throat. *I'm a dead man if I can't pick up another lead before Bruno or the Terrans catch up with me.*

"Tell you what, kid," Wirst said after a few moments. "You go down to the beach house and enjoy that little gal, and I'll get this ship ready to fly again. I'll look over the computer records from your last visit here and see if I can figure out where you went, and you can go from there."

"Where I went? You can't track a point-to-point jump, Wirst," Rake said exasperatedly.

"Who said you jumped?" Wirst countered. "You said you died here. Your ship's still gotta be here somewhere, right?"

Rake's frown vanished, and he felt like an idiot. "Of course it does. Thanks, Wirst." He started to walk away, then stopped and looked back. "What do you mean, 'enjoy that little gal'?"

The old mechanic just laughed as he walked away.

IX

RAKE DIDN'T HAVE THE PATIENCE to sit around and wait - not with the underworld and the only remaining superpower in the Expanse both eager to get their hands on him. Staying in one place seemed to be a great way to let a skiptracer catch up to him and splatter his brains all over the ground. *Again.*

He had just managed to get the engines of an airskimmer running with some creative short-circuiting on the ignition board when he sensed a presence. Turning his head, he saw a familiar pair of dainty booted feet. "Meg," he grunted, returning his attention to closing up the ignition panel.

"Where are you off to? Blow up my home, then dump me on the first planet we come to?" the young woman asked bluntly, her tone heated. "What happened to talking to me before you disappeared?"

"I doubt I'm going to be hitting the spacelanes with an airskimmer, Meg," Rake grunted. "Until Wirst has the *Starfall* patched up, I'm not going too far."

"Uh-huh. Then why are you going anywhere at all?"

"I need to get some work done and check some leads."

"Leads? What leads?"

Rake immediately regretted his choice of words. He finished with the ignition, satisfied that it wouldn't shut down mid-flight, and straightened up. Instead of answering Meg, he seated himself firmly in the pilot's seat and began strapping in.

The girl apparently wouldn't take a hint. As Rake began drawing the safety straps over his shoulders, Meg vaulted into the passenger seat behind Rake and mimicked his motions.

"Meg," Rake said firmly, "get out of the airskimmer. I don't have time for this."

The girl didn't answer with words; instead, she firmly snapped her safety restraints in place and then reached up to jerk the canopy closed.

The pilot sighed and shut up as he glanced over the monitors. Engines, stabilizers, flight computer, power levels all showed a glowing friendly green. He didn't bother with words as he fed power to the ionic lifters.

The airskimmer was in rough shape as it lifted vertically from the ground, swaying left and right as the flight computer tried to stabilize the little craft.

Sensors must be dinged up, he concluded. *Garbage input, garbage output. In this case, a rough flight.* A faint smile touched his lips. *Any flight is better than sitting around on the ground, anyway.*

When the little vessel was thirty meters off the ground, he began directing energy to the main drives. The airskimmer steadily picked up speed, and he dialed back the lifters as more traditional aerodynamics took over and forward momentum kept the skimmer aloft.

Rake kept a steady hand on the controls as they bounced through the air. It wasn't a smooth flight as the computers struggled to keep the craft properly stabilized sans reliable data; several times the ride was rough enough that he was tempted to disable the stabilization and take full control of the airskimmer manually. On the other hand, when he glanced in the cockpit mirror and saw Meg's green visage in the back seat, he decided he could tolerate the bouncing ride.

Serves her right for deciding to tag along.

Clarion boasted only a single major city, New Ziric, which hosted a starport more fit for a major population center like Terra than a sparsely-populated outer colony. In spite of its clientele - Rake would be considered too law-abiding to be trustworthy, given he had no dead-or-alive bounties on his head - the place was large, clean, well-kept, and carefully maintained. Order reigned, though it wasn't quite as ordered as the central worlds. Rather, New Ziric functioned by a single rule: keep your business to yourself.

Travelers who broke that rule, should they survive, were not welcome to return.

The flight took well over two hours, and Rake spent most of it in silence. When the port was visible on the horizon, however, Rake finally broke the silence. "You should've stayed at Wirst's and enjoyed the beach," he commented. "I guarantee Caree and her crew are having a great time, and I bet they would've loved to have a barkeep on hand to make it even better."

Meg gave him a glare that could have cracked the cockpit mirror. "What, I should just sit on the beach and bury my toes and my head in the sand? You dragged me into this, and I'm not letting you abandon me, even if this *is* a beautiful world." She shuddered. "Besides, I'm having trouble with all this...space."

Rake frowned as he began to shed speed and altitude. "What do you mean?"

"You're a pilot," she grumbled. "You spend most of your time in a ship, don't you? Doesn't it bother you when you park on some planet and go walking around outside?"

Rake could have smacked himself.

She's spent almost all of her life in close quarters. She's never had to deal with this kind of open space. He looked out through the airskimmer's canopy with a new respect. *That could be...disconcerting.* He glanced back in the mirror again. *She's probably not sick from the flight, you idiot, she's trying to deal with being in the open air.*

"Actually, when you're the guy flying, you get used to nothing *but* open space," Rake commented. "Space is huge and empty. You get used to having nothing but clear sky around you."

Meg shuddered.

The entire port island was about ten kilometers across and almost perfectly round. Rake didn't bother radioing ahead for any sort of clearance; no planets this far out worried about air traffic, beyond keeping skimmers out of the descent corridors for incoming starships. In this case, the skimmer's flight computer was programmed with a map of the entire port island, including approved parking structures for airskimmers.

As the craft descended toward one of the parking zones in the center of the island, he browsed through more of the map's information. Before he was forced to turn his concentration back to the landing, he found two shops that could fulfill his immediate needs.

Landing was even rougher than the takeoff and flight had been; the starboard lifter sputtered as Rake attempted to set down, and the flight computer struggled to keep the skimmer level. Two meters above the parking garage floor, the starboard lifter failed entirely, and the skimmer crashed with a teeth-rattling impact.

After confirming both he and Meg were alive and relatively intact, he unstrapped and slid the canopy open. Curiosity made him scramble under the craft to check the lifter, and he grimaced when he saw the corrosion build-up.

No wonder the ionics were stuttering, he thought irritably. *Let these things rust, and soon they won't work at all. Really, it's amazing this thing got us off the ground in the first place.* He swallowed as another thought occurred to him. *Of course, that might be why Wirst had it parked in the first place.*

"So, now where to?" the still-green Meg asked Rake as she clumsily dropped from the cockpit.

"First, I need some clothes," Rake grumbled. "I'm tired of wearing whatever someone else gives me. And I need a decent gun."

"And then what?"

"Wait and see."

* * *

Thirty minutes later, Rake stepped out of a shop, feeling much more comfortable. A brown leather jacket replaced the shredded one he'd left behind on the *Starfall.* Properly fitted, knee-high boots were a bit stiffer than he'd prefer, but that was a temporary discomfort that would pass as soon as they were properly broken in. A nicely-worn but well-maintained pistol had slipped neatly into his holster and felt nearly as natural as his long-lost sidearm. A wide-brimmed hat completed his outfit - plain and a darker brown than his new jacket. When he had time and had recovered his own ship, he would add the other accoutrements he preferred to carry in his clothes.

Meg had grown increasingly jittery as he had refitted himself. She had managed to stay quiet through the entire ordeal, but her impatient looks were obvious, and her foot seemed to tap of its own accord.

When she stepped out of the shop, she finally asked, "So, what now?"

"You're not big into surprises, are you?" Rake asked with a grin.

"No," she said bluntly.

"You can always go wait back at the airskimmer," he offered.

"That sounds like a worse idea than following you around."

"I didn't ask you to come," he rebutted. "You made that decision all on your own."

"Damned straight I did. And I'm *deciding* to follow you a while longer," she retorted. "So, now what?"

"Now, we're going to visit an old friend," Rake said, stepping out onto the plain fused-stone sidewalk. His pace wasn't hurried, but his long legs ate up distance easily, and Meg nearly had to break into a jog to keep up.

"Oh? What old friend?"

Rake rolled his eyes. "When you were running your pub on the ring, did pilots coming through always tell you everything you asked them?"

"Yes."

That nearly caused Rake to break stride.

Actually, that makes sense, he thought. *Lot of people talk to barkeeps - especially if they're young, impressionable girls. That's a habit I need to break myself from.*

"Well, it's a good thing you're not running a pub anymore," he said with a smile.

"Why didn't you ask Caree to come along?" Meg asked after a moment had passed. "She seems like she'd be good backup if this gets ugly."

"I'm not planning on this getting rough," Rake replied placidly. "This should be a nice, quick trip. No shooting involved."

Meg fell into a pensive quiet, still barely keeping up with Rake's long strides. Rake opened his mouth to comfort her twice and stopped himself both times.

Let her be nervous. She needs to figure out what these outer worlds are like - especially if she can't go back to Lantash.

The old traffic control tower was exactly as Rake had remembered it, though on second glance he thought it might have fallen into even further disrepair. Paint and rust competed for surface area, with the paint clearly losing the battle. Most of the glass was long since shattered, exposing the interior to the relatively mild weather of the island. Still, as Rake pushed the door open, he noted the floor was covered with debris - sand, twigs, and leaves primarily, but other detritus wasn't so easily identified.

Rake disregarded it all as irrelevant, walked past the no-doubt broken elevator, and started up the stairs. The staircase wound around the long elevator shaft, vanishing into darkness above. The pilot sighed as he started up. *Just as wonderful as I remembered it.*

"So, why are we climbing up an abandoned tower?" Meg asked breathlessly.

"Because you decided to follow me," Rake replied.

"Very funny. So why are *you* climbing an abandoned tower?"

"I need the exercise," he said, irritation starting to creep into his tone.

Meg, thankfully, took the hint and followed up the steps in silence.

Rake didn't stop to rest during the climb; instead, he pressed on to the top, though he was sweating profusely by the time he reached the door at the summit. Meg doubled over as soon as they stopped, clutching her sides and gasping for air.

The pilot knew he was hurting nearly as bad as the girl, but didn't show it. He did allow himself to lean against the door while swallowing lungfuls of air, doing his best to ignore the stitches in his side. When he finally felt as though he could speak without gasping, he knocked on the door.

For several moments, there was no response. Then a voice spoke from a speaker overhead. Rake looked up to see the little grey box, hanging from its two wires. "Who are you?"

"It's me, Weston," Rake said. "Open the door, old man."

"Weston? He's dead," the voice said. "Go away before I fill you full of holes."

The pilot glanced around and saw several rusted tubes subtly rotate to point in his direction. "I had an insurance policy," Rake said. "Now open the door. I can't afford another one."

"What's the password?" the speaker demanded.

"The password is *open the damn door before I kick it down and shoot you*," he answered sweetly. "Your choice."

The door swung open, and a grey-haired man stuck his head out, looking Rake up and down. "What the hell are you doing here? You were dead only a few days ago, right here."

Rake pushed his way past the old man and into the tower. "That's why I'm here. I have no idea how I died, and I've got both the Terrans and Boss Bruno gunning for me."

"And you came *here?* Thanks, Weston - that's what I really need. I should kick you out right now! Wait, who has the bigger reward for your head? I might as well make a profit on this deal."

The room was nearly as derelict as the rest of the tower, but that was due to the empty wrappers and plastic containers scattered across the floor. The computer equipment mounted along the walls and under the massive windows was all neatly maintained and glowed with power and activity lights. Rake found a chair, upended it to rid it of its collection of debris, and then seated himself. "Beats me, though the Terrans have been the ones shooting at me. They dropped nukes on the ring out at Lantash to flush me out."

"What did you get yourself into, boy?" the old man asked.

"Excuse me," Meg interrupted from the door. "Who is this?"

The old man looked at Rake. "Who is this?" he echoed.

"Meg, this is Shoram, the best data broker on the planet." Rake glanced at the girl. "Shoram, this is Meg, the barkeep from the ring."

"Seems kind of excessive to bring a barkeep with you," Shoram observed. "Most people are content to visit them from time to time in their establishments."

"Well, it seemed like the thing to do, given the Terrans were doing their best to fill her hole up with rocks," Rake replied. "I haven't been able to get rid of her since."

"Not for lack of trying," Meg grumbled.

"So, what information are you looking for?" Shoram asked, returning his attention to Rake.

"Any official information on how I got killed, and any flight data you can find on my ship," Rake said promptly. "I know the *where* is here, and I'm pretty sure my ship has to be nearby somewhere."

"So really, you're not looking for flight data on the ship - you're looking for the ship itself," Shoram clarified.

Rake grunted an affirmative.

"I've already got the information on your death," Shoram said. "I actually read all the reports from it yesterday, after I heard you'd been killed." He shook his head. "No mention of you having an insurance policy, though, and nothing there to even suggest it. I was a bit surprised to see you come walking up to my door."

"Wait a minute," Rake said as he started to connect dots, "was I here before? As in, in the last week?"

Shoram nodded. "Yes. You asked me to keep an eye on incoming traffic and alert you if I saw any Terran craft come down-planet."

"Why would you bother?" Meg asked skeptically. "Any decent ship computer could flag incoming official transponders."

"They could, but I wasn't just looking for official transponders, girl," Shoram said bluntly. "You think all Terran craft are flying the flag and announcing who they are? Are you really that naive?"

Meg blushed bright red, and started to reply when Rake cut her off. "And what did you see?"

"No Terrans arrived here before you died," Shoram said. "Fifteen hours after, yes, there was one transport with a team on it, but they were way too late to nail you. I didn't know you were dead at the time, of course, so I tried to call you but got no answer."

"So Boss Bruno's crew nailed me," Rake mused.

"You're assuming there's not a third party in the works," the old man pointed out helpfully. "You know about two players, but that doesn't mean there's *only* two players."

"Thank you for the helpful reminder," the pilot groused.

"I've got the information on your death here," Shoram said as he shuffled over to a console stacked high with paper. "Right...oh, where did I put that?" He rummaged through reams of paper for several moments before finally extracting a thin stack of printouts. "Here. Autopsy reports, local authority reports, and a copy of the transmission from the Terrans two hours after they landed."

"If they were Terrans, wouldn't their radio be encrypted?" Meg asked skeptically.

"Do you ever get tired of being wrong, girl?" Shoram asked. "Of *course* it was encrypted. That's why I had to decrypt it."

"And how did you do that?"

"Look at what you're surrounded with," he said impatiently.

"I see a lot of old equipment that doesn't have the horsepower to do all this data cracking," she retorted.

"Shoram is a lot smarter than he looks," Rake offered.

"Hey!" the old man objected. "I don't look…"

"The reason he's set up in this old tower is because the locals never bothered disconnecting it from the master data grids," Rake explained casually. "As long as he's got that hardware line in, he's good enough he can hack anything."

"It's a lot easier decrypting when I can use the city's system to do the lifting," Shoram finally relented. "Enough processing power to brute-force crack all their own encryptions."

Meg shook her head in disbelief, but finally fell silent.

"So, do you know where my ship is?" Rake asked.

The data broker shook his head. "I might be able to find it, but you had me bouncing the data you wanted off a satellite and back down. You said you were running silent with no transmissions, so I can't easily back trace it."

"But you can find it?"

"Boy, finding things is *what I do*," he said indignantly. "That's why people pay me. It may take a day or two, though."

"And what will it cost me to make it your top priority?"

"Triple my usual fee," the old man grinned.

"You're going to drain my accounts dry," Rake complained.

"Yes, but at least you'll still be alive to refill them," Shoram said. "Deal?"

"Do it," Rake said.

"Good." The man turned his back on both Rake and Meg as he shuffled over to the bank of computers in the center of the room. "I should have something in a couple hours. Stop back then."

* * *

As the pair descended the stairs, Meg couldn't seem to shut up. "Why didn't you negotiate? How do you even know what he'll charge you?"

"Shoram has standard rates. No negotiating." Rake tried to tamp down his impatience and the fear starting to niggle at the back of his mind.

"*Everyone* negotiates," Meg objected.

"Not everyone. Some people are good enough that you pay their price. It's not like he's hard up for cash; he's got a list of contracts as long as my leg," the pilot said.

"Contracts? For who?"

"Lots of crime lords, a few pirate chiefs," Rake said offhand. "Those are mostly for keeping track of the coming and going of certain people of interest, or particular cargoes. The real illegal contracts are with government officials, though."

"What? Why?"

Rake allowed himself a small smile. "Because crime syndicates are amateurs compared to governments when it comes to the illegal."

"So what now?" Meg asked.

"Now, we find somewhere to lie low for a few hours while Shoram gets us the information we need."

"I'm guessing you're not planning on flying back to Wirst's island," Meg noted.

"Nope, got another stop I need to make - and it'll definitely take a few hours."

✕

RAKE STUMBLED A BIT AS he walked out of the clinic. Meg caught his arm and helped steady him, but he didn't stop walking.

"I can't believe you did that," the girl said, her expression still as stunned as when Rake had led her into the building.

"Why?" he asked.

She shuddered in revulsion. "You let them cut you open and put *machines* inside! Machines should always be on the *outside*, not the inside!"

Rake couldn't help but laugh. "You sound like you grew up on some barely-settled world, not Lantash."

"What's that supposed to mean?" Meg demanded indignantly.

"Most pilots have implants," he said calmly. "It's easier if you can feed the data straight to your brain without having to look at all the controls and gauges."

"Aren't you worried about your brain being hacked?" Meg asked nervously. "I mean, you can plug yourself into most computer systems. I've heard horror stories of people catching computer viruses and winding up as vegetables!"

"They're just stories, Meg," he said, striving to keep the amusement out of his tone. "You know why I'm not worried about it?"

"Why?" she asked suspiciously.

"Because everyone's brain is different," he explained. "Everyone is wired differently. It's why insurance policies are expensive and can only be managed by professionals - they have to monitor the brain as it grows in the tank to ensure it'll be compatible with the dump they took of the original brain. It's also why they couldn't, say, grow a copy of one of the Terran councilors and put my memories in the body - the physical brain's individual synapses just aren't close enough to make it work."

"So how does that protect your brain from being hacked?" she asked, some of her revulsion replaced by curiosity.

"Because while all brains run on the same basic principles, the actual connections are unique in every head. Given enough time - a few months, or maybe even years - I don't doubt someone could hack my head. But that would only have allowed them to hack *my* brain, not yours or my brother's or anyone else's. It would take an enormous amount of effort for almost no gain."

"If it's so unique, then what good does it do? I mean, it's not like you'll be able to hook up to any computer and use it that way, right?"

"Right," he said approvingly. "*But*, with some time, you can calibrate a computer system to work with your own brain. There's not a lot of practical use for it, unless you're a hacker and using your own system to sift data from remote computers, *or* if you're a pilot with your own ship." He smiled at Meg. "When I'm on my own ship, and I plug in, I can *see* using the sensors, navigate by instinct, and fly with faster reflexes than anyone using physical controls."

"But only on your ship."

"Only on my ship," he agreed with a nod. "A lot of independent pilots and the Terran military all have neural hookups for that reason. On the Terran side, it allows pilots to communicate faster than verbalizing speech, even though most of them don't like that part of it."

"Why?" she asked with a frown. "Wouldn't it give them an edge in combat?"

"Yes, it would," Rake agreed. "For that matter, so would using the same technology for every position on a warship. But most people, even soldiers, prefer being alone in their brains." He shrugged. "There's downsides, too - you can start feeding negative feelings into the communications network, and they start growing on each other, and pretty soon an entire squadron or warship crew is demoralized."

"Huh. I hadn't thought of that," Meg confessed.

"Most people don't," Rake said with a smile. "Anyway, I needed this if I'm going to use my ship. I actually have a number of the systems locked so a neural link is necessary to access their data."

"So now back to your hacker friend?" she wanted to know.

"One more stop first," he contradicted. "Besides, he's probably not done crunching the information."

"So where to next?"

"Wait and see."

* * *

"What are we doing here?" Meg muttered as they walked through the sliding door.

"Shopping," Rake said with a humorless grin. "I thought you'd appreciate that."

The girl snorted. "Yeah, I spent my whole life traveling to stores in the Lantash Six ring and buying all sorts of frivolous things. Oh, wait, I *didn't*."

Rake shook his head. "When I get my ship back, I'm going to need some equipment. With all the trouble following me around, I don't want to take any chances with either the Terrans or Boss Bruno."

"What sort of equipment are you looking for here, then?" she asked dubiously.

"Why the hundred questions?" the pilot groused. "It doesn't matter to you, does it?"

"Hey, I'm just trying to make conversation," she shot back. "I'd rather I didn't just walk around like your silent shadow; thought you'd like to talk to someone."

"I *like* silence," Rake said firmly. "I'm more than content with silence. That's why I was going to come over here alone, not with a girl who has no idea what's going on in the world."

Meg fell into an angry silence. Rake was grateful for the silence now descending on his ears. *Nice and peaceful,* he thought as he walked through the shop, glancing through the aisles with an eye out for a salesman.

It took less than two minutes for a well-dressed girl, perhaps a few years older than Meg, to offer her assistance. She was cute in her way - shoulder-length hair dyed deep green, accenting her green eyes and perfectly matching her evergreen lips. *Gene-modified,* Rake observed distantly. *Not that it matters to me.*

"Can I help you, sir?" she asked him.

"I'm looking for a top-notch pilot AI," Rake said casually. "What do you have in stock?"

She offered him a smile, revealing a matching set of green teeth. "We have several pilot AIs in stock," she said brightly. "Depending on your needs, we have everything from a basic straight-flight AI requiring manual takeoffs, landings, and re-entries to a full-fledged AI that includes point-to-point navigation and launch-landing routines good for twenty worlds."

"What about combat AIs?" he asked, dropping his voice and ignoring the strangled gasp from Meg.

The sales girl's volume dropped to match Rake's tone. "With or without full weapons control?" she asked.

"Without."

"We have two models, the Cee-One and the Cee-Six. The Cee-One is a full AI capable of running anything up to and including a frigate. It offers full tracking and target prediction services, and is the best we have available. While you're not looking for automated weapons control, the Cee-One is capable of it with an optional add-on package.

"The Cee-Six was designed as a pilot support AI for a fighter, and is optimized for high-speed, high-agility maneuvers in complete vacuum. It is capable of atmospheric flight operations and handling craft as large as a gunship, but it's not the best solution for such a craft." The girl in green offered another emerald smile. "Are you interested in either of these? It will be at least another week before we have other AIs in stock."

"What sort of package do these AIs come in?" Rake asked. "Full robot body or just an AI box?"

"We've found most end users who want full-motion capability in their AIs prefer a custom shell," the sales girl said. "Rather than burden both ourselves and our customers with the extra cost, we sell all our AIs as a box. Of course, we have shells available here if you're looking for one of those as well."

"Just a box for now," Rake said as he mused his options over. "How capable is the Cee-One in something the size of a fighter, anyway? If I have something that size, would I be better off with the Six?"

"Cee-Ones are fully capable in a fighter," the girl confirmed. "The Cee-Two through Cee-Six lines are actually subsets of the Cee-One, with their code trimmed and optimized for particular platforms. In this case, if you're flying a fighter, the Cee-One will be just as capable as a Cee-Six, but the Cee-Six will run less than half the cost."

"If I need to plug a Cee-Six into something bigger, can it handle the load?" Rake asked, ignoring the fidgeting Meg who clearly wanted to speak up.

"The bigger the ship, the less combat-effective a Cee-Six AI will be," the sales girl warned. "In theory, they could manage very basic navigation of a frigate, for example, but it will hardly be combat-capable. It just doesn't have the software or the necessary processing power for a ship that big."

Rake nodded slowly. "What's your opinion? Is the Cee-One worth the extra cash?"

"Depends on your ship," the girl said. "From what my customers have told me, anything bigger than, say, a gunship, and the Cee-Six's effectiveness falls dramatically. Anything smaller, and the Cee-Six's optimization is about equal to a Cee-One's broader capabilities." She smiled slyly and offered a wink. "The Cee-One's a better option if you think you'll be trading up ships in the future."

She probably thinks I'm a pirate, Rake realized. *Of course, most people coming in here and asking about combat AIs probably* are *pirates…or at the very least, don't have* legal *intentions for any AI they buy.* He hid the smile that tried to betray his dispassionate bargaining persona. *Then again, are my intentions legal? Probably not.*

"I'll take the Cee-Six," he decided aloud. "For thirty percent less than what you're asking," he added.

Ten minutes of bargaining and feature-discussion ended with Rake paying eighty-two percent of the sticker price. "And would you like us to install it on your ship and ensure its full compatibility?" she asked as she ran the charge against the account Rake had provided.

"No, I'll take it with me," he said firmly.

She eyed him openly. "Not very many people walk around with an AI box under their arm," she commented.

"My ship isn't here," he explained briefly.

She probably thinks I'm going to be stealing a ship and using the AI to fly it out of here. It's not a bad idea, actually; if I'd get desperate enough, that might make a good plan. With a decent AI to override the security systems, I bet it would work.

She offered another green smile, but her tone was professional and cautious. "Yes, sir. Please remember that, while self-install will not void the warranty, opening the AI box will make it ineligible for free repair or return."

Rake grunted at the standard phrasing. "Yeah, I know the drill," he said. "Anything else?"

"Have you had an AI before?" she asked helpfully.

"Not a new AI, no - I've had a few used ones that were already integrated with ship systems."

"As the first owner, you'll need to set security codes and a designation for your new AI," the sales girl supplied. "With some AIs, you'll have the option of choosing a personality, but the Cee line does not have any options available but the stock setup."

"Standard stuff," Rake said with a slow nod. "Anything else I need to know?"

The sales girl shook his head. "Your ship should have all the information you need to integrate the AI into your systems," she continued seamlessly. "If your ship is, for whatever reason, missing the owner's manual, you should be able to find the information available on the ComNet. If, for whatever reason, you cannot find the information on the ComNet, I would recommend contacting your vessel's manufacturer."

Rake rolled his eyes as she continued through her spiel.

"You can return the AI for a full refund within ninety days for a fifteen percent restocking fee, assuming there is no sign of tampering with the AI's physical box. If it needs warranty service, it can be returned to Automated Industries via any authorized service provider, including this shop."

Rake waved off the rest of it. "Standard terms, I get it," he said smoothly. "Thank you."

The AI box wasn't very large - the standard sized fifteen centimeters per side, in a perfect cube. The AI was heavy for its size, packed solidly with circuits and memory - enough so it was uncomfortable to carry by fingertip.

Rake settled for tucking it under his arm as he walked out of the shop, Meg in tow.

They were barely clear of the doors when the girl started talking again. "Aren't you some sort of hotshot pilot?" Meg asked.

Rake rolled his eyes. "Some sort, yes," he allowed. *If you only had some idea of the hell I've seen and done*, he thought. *Then you wouldn't ask such stupid questions.*

"If you're a great pilot, like all the rumors I heard on the ring, then why would you bother buying a pilot AI to fly for you?" she inquired. "I mean, it seems like it'd be a step backward. Everything I've heard says a pilot AI is inferior to a flesh-and-blood pilot."

Rake didn't immediately respond - he already knew why he had bought the AI, but he wasn't sure he wanted anyone else to know.

Or do I know why I bought it? he wondered. *I grabbed it as a backup for the ship, right?*

Rake grimaced as he thought about it.

No, that wasn't the reason. Well, not the only reason. You're worried about your reflexes and this damned body, aren't you? Afraid it's going to fall apart on you and that you won't be able to fly the ship? He swallowed hard. *That's the truth, isn't it? You're losing your edge, and you're so afraid of it that you'll resort to an AI to try to stay ahead of it.*

Are my skills already that far gone?

He looked down at his hands, studying them as though the first time he had seen them. They looked a bit different than all the memories he had - a body grown for an insurance policy lacked, by necessity, all the breaks and scars of the original. There was no perceptible shake, but they felt unsteady nonetheless.

No, they aren't - not yet, anyway. This body may be failing, but it hasn't failed yet.

Rake took a steadying breath.

Maybe you did buy this pilot AI because you're afraid and you know things aren't in your favor. That doesn't mean it's not true.

Aloud, he finally answered Meg's question. "My ship needs a couple crewman to operate at peak efficiency. Usually I'm fine flying it solo, but there are too many people looking for my head right now to risk that. If I let a combat AI fly the ship and monitor the onboard systems, I can concentrate on manning the weapons."

"Why not let the AI use the guns, too?" Meg asked.

"Because a Cee-Six AI isn't capable of using the weapons independently," Rake answered. "You'd have to get something in the Teens line to handle the guns, too, and it would've cost twice what a Cee-One AI runs."

"Still, wouldn't it be better for you to fly and an AI to shoot?" Meg persisted. "I mean, you said yourself you fly better than an AI."

"It's safer to let an AI pilot and me to shoot than the other way around."

"Why?"

Rake rolled his eyes. "Always why, why, why with you," he commented. "Too many questions."

"Then just answer this one," Meg pestered.

"An AI is only as good as a ship's sensors and its own software package," Rake reluctantly answered. "And during the Great War, and ever since, militaries and pirates and smugglers have all put a lot of money into finding ways to jam or disrupt accurate sensor data - for the primary purpose of stopping an AI from accurately tracking and shooting at them. With all that in mind, it sounds like a way better idea to let the AI fly the ship while *I* shoot, not the other way around."

The girl nodded, apparently satisfied with the answer. "So, you just want to make sure you're combat-ready when the Terrans or Bruno's people come gunning for you."

"Exactly."

"So does that mean you're going to leave Caree's crew and me behind when you find your ship?"

Rake steadied the heavy little AI box under his arm before answering. "Not exactly. I was pretty sure both you and Caree would want to be clear of whatever the hell mess I'm in. Hanging around with me too long is a good way to get yourself killed."

Meg snorted. "You already brought this whole thing down on my head, and now you're going to run off before you have to cut any of us in on the payoff, aren't you? Pretty low, Weston."

"Payoff?" Rake asked dumbly.

"You've got a government and a crime lord both chasing you *after you already died*," she said irritably. "There has to be a payoff involved here. No one would chase you *past your death* just to drop you on a prison planet, or to kill you again. Everyone's chasing you for the payoff, and I'll be damned if you're going to cut me out of the loop after you blew up my pub."

"I didn't blow up your pub," he protested.

"No, but you sure brought the people who did, didn't you? Because of *your* attempt to run and hide, my comfortable little establishment is now filled to the brim with rock and will need to be excavated - if there's enough left of the refueling station there to even be worth it. So no, you're not going to cut me out of the loop." She snorted at the dumbfounded pilot. "You can't possibly think Caree is going to cut and run, either. If she were going to do that, she would've called the authorities in herself, or at the very least dropped you off here on Clarion and burned sky."

Rake blew out a long sigh.

At least I don't have to worry about them ditching me - for now, anyway. Just wish I knew what payday it was that we were chasing.

"Well," he said, changing the subject, "Let's see what Shoram managed to dig up on my ship."

XI

THE SKIES WERE DARK AND overcast by the time Rake and Meg returned to Shoram's tower.

On Terra or any of the earlier settled worlds, they'd have weather control, Rake observed distantly. *Out here, though, they just let the atmosphere do whatever the hell it wants.*

Meg was quiet as they climbed the stairs up to Shoram's nest at the top of the tower. Whether it was because she had nothing to say, or merely because she was so out of breath she couldn't talk, Rake didn't know, but he was nonetheless grateful for the reprieve on his ears.

At the top, he pounded on the door but didn't wait for Shoram to answer before swinging the door open.

"Coming, coming," the old man called hurriedly from somewhere out of Rake's field of vision. "Just a minute."

"C'mon, old man, I'm paying you plenty for this," Rake answered. "I need the information so I can find my ship."

"Your ship is hardly running away, Weston," Shoram replied acidly from somewhere out of sight. A moment later, a fake wall slid open and Shoram stepped through, his hair soaking wet.

"So, what did you find?" the pilot asked. "Do you know where my ship is, or not?"

The old data broker glared at him. "Young man, don't you have any respect for me? I have to work *hard* to put these pieces together, and you never have time to be grateful. It's really quite a shame that you won't spend any time appreciating just what I do for you."

"C'mon, old man," Rake said impatiently. "Did you find it or not?"

"Weston, what I do doesn't work that way. It's not a binary choice, a yes-or-no answer." Shoram shook his head in frustration with the pilot. "It's percentages - probabilities and likelihoods, not yes-or-no."

"Either you found my ship, or you didn't," the pilot said irritably.

"I *may* have found your ship," Shoram allowed. "I may not have."

"So why am I giving you exorbitant amounts of money?"

"Patience, boy. Do you expect a woman to give you all her secrets immediately as well?"

"If I'm paying her, absolutely," Rake declared.

Shoram shook his head. "Young people. No patience, no appreciation."

"Well?" the pilot said, tapping his foot.

The old data broker flipped two switches. The first shut off the tower's internal lights, dropping the room into a gloom only broken by the glow from his processing equipment and the dim light filtering through the observation windows from the cloudy skies. The second kicked on an overhead projector, making the entire floor glow with a blue sheen.

Rake stared down at the floor, and it took a moment before he realized it wasn't just illumination - it was a flattened map of all of Clarion, with the predominant color as light blue from the vast oceans that covered the world.

"Clarion," the man said with a small smile, "is a big place. Even though it has far larger oceans than any other world in the Expanse, it's difficult to search. I could not assume you had, after all, parked your ship on dry land. Modern spacecraft would be capable of submersion without breach, though I can't imagine it would do anything good for the engines. Given who was chasing you, it was conceivable you dumped your ship in the ocean to ensure it wouldn't be found by your pursuers."

"Did I?" Rake asked.

Shoram ignored the question, clearly caught up in the moment and unperturbed by the pilot's impatience. "Of course, I also could assume that you would eventually hope to recover your ship, so it was unlikely you would have submerged it too deeply and risked the oceans crushing it. Therefore, I could rule out the deeper oceans and concentrate my efforts on the shallower waters near any of the existing islands, as well as known shallow spots where there was no island actually protruding above the water. There are a surprising number of those here on Clarion."

Rake clamped down hard on his impatience.

"Because there is little law here, there are no traffic control satellites overhead," the data broker continued, "which means there is no accurate trajectory data for your ship when you arrived on Clarion. The primary spaceport here has such data, but it is only accurate for a few hundred kilometers around the island, give or take another hundred kilometers for the altitude of the ship in question."

"What about surveillance satellites?" Meg asked. Rake turned to glare at the girl for interrupting, but she ignored him in turn.

"Alas, there are no official surveillance satellites, either," Shoram said sadly.

"Official?" Meg echoed.

Yellow lines began to trace across the projected floor-map. "What Clarion *does* have is a number of communication satellites," he said with a twinkle in his eye. "They are necessary, of course, to allow communication between locations around the curvature of the planet, as well as to connect us out to the broader ComNet. Those communication satellites do tell us a story of sorts about your ship, Rake."

The pilot gritted his teeth, resisting the urge to throttle the old man until he gave up the location of the freighter.

"You had initially arrived here at the spaceport, then departed but did not leave the planet," Shoram continued. On the floor projection, the primary spaceport glowed a bright red contrast to the blue oceans. "Two and a half hours later, according to the traffic control logs, you returned aboard an airskimmer, which, given the speed of the skimmer, gives us a radius to search. Granted, that still amounts to something like a fifteen percent of the surface area of the planet, but it's a starting point." A wide circle of the ocean swapped from blue to green on the floor, indicating the travel range of the skimmer.

"So you narrowed down the area my ship is parked in to, what, seventy-five million square kilometers?" Rake snorted, and sarcasm dripped from his words. "I should be able to search that in a day or two, right?"

"Given our other parameters, including the assumption you would recover your ship, we're actually down to about five million square kilometers," the old man said reprovingly. "And I didn't stop there."

Rake ground his teeth in frustration.

"You were using a data feed while you were flying out to wherever it was you parked your ship," Shoram continued placidly. "And as you traveled, you bounced between three satellites, which gives us a rough trajectory you were flying - within a corridor perhaps a hundred kilometers wide, of course, and also assuming you flew directly to your ship's final resting place, rather than a roundabout path."

That drew Rake's attention. "So you know where I was flying, then."

Shoram nodded. "And I know which satellite your ship was last in connection with while pulling data. Now, Clarion's satellite grid is a mess of sorts - it's not properly geosynchronous, and there are frequently gaps in coverage while satellites double-up in other areas. Backtracking the satellite orbits with the best probabilities I can manage, I put the odds of your ship being here, at Windward Island, at seventy-three percent."

The tiny, rocky island glowed bright pink.

"Seventy-three percent," Rake mused.

"I dropped the decimal - I doubted you'd be interested in such minutiae," Shoram offered.

"What's around there?" Meg asked. "Any settlers or smaller spaceports or anything like that?"

The data broker shook his head. "Windward Island is pretty much a large boulder, with almost no vegetation. Some of the islands nearby are in its shadow and are softer and could support settlements, but no one has established anything out there yet."

"What do you mean, in its shadow?" the girl asked.

"Weather patterns on the planet," the old man explained. "Storms predominantly move from west to east. Windward Island is fairly large - several hundred kilometers across. There are several smaller islands that exist in its storm shadow. While they still receive adequate rainfall, they are spared the worst of the wind and the waves."

"We should be able to get out there within an hour on the airskimmer I took from Wirst," Rake commented. "Time to get moving."

"Good luck," the old man said. "I hope you succeed." He shut the floor projector off, and the room plunged into darkness.

Even with the cloud cover, it wasn't that dark out, was it? Rake wondered for a moment as his eyes tried to adjust to the gloom.

Rain was beginning to fall, pitter-patter against the observation windows, and it nearly obscured the view outside.

Nearly.

Rake still managed to make out the hulking image of a Terran gunship.

"Down!" he shouted, turning to tackle Meg to the floor.

Shoram wasn't fast enough.

The gunship's cannons opened up, spraying the room with projectiles. The observation windows shattered, computer equipment died amidst a storm of dancing sparks, and smoke rolled from riddled processing equipment.

Meg screamed and struggled, but Rake held her down tightly to the floor.

Best chance of surviving is to stay down until they cease fire, then *make a run for it.*

Shoram hit the floor next to them with a dull, heavy thump that left no doubt he was dead. Warm, sticky wetness splattered across Rake's face, and he told himself it was surely rain, because the alternative was too distracting if he intended to survive the next few minutes.

The gunfire from the Terran warship seemed to last a millennia, a rhythmic *pachoo-pachoo-pachoo* from the coilguns that was as constant as a steady rainfall. Fear gripped Rake, but he clung tightly to Meg and the floor, waiting for an opportunity.

An eternity later, the coilguns stopped. Rake dared to look up, saw magnetic lines shooting through the broken viewports and snapping into place inside the tower. "Run!" he shouted to Meg, rolling off her and scrambling to his feet. "Run, don't stop!"

In a moment of clarity, he realized his earlier mistake during his first meeting with Shoram. He had asked the old man if the Terrans had pursued him to Clarion the first time, a few days prior, but he had never asked the old man if the Terrans had *left* the planet.

Meg had barely made it to her feet when the door slammed open.

Rake whirled on the door and drew his sidearm, the motion liquid-smooth, and he was firing before he was consciously aware of it.

The first two men in Terran commando gear, clad head to toe in light body armor, went down in the first second. The rest of the squad took up cover outside the door immediately.

Rake gritted his teeth. *Trapped. Only one thing to do.*

He tossed his gun down. The sidearm bounced with a loud clatter, and Rake shouted to make himself heard. "We surrender!" he called. "We surrender!"

The Terrans at the door didn't immediately leave their cover. Meg shot him a betrayed look, but he merely shook his head at her. *They've got us, and trying to fight our way out would get us killed.*

He wondered for just a moment what the Terran commandos were waiting for when a trio of loud thumps behind him signaled the arrival of more soldiers through the shattered viewports. *Of course - why leave cover when you've got more firepower coming in to cover your back?*

The pilot turned slowly, his hands in the air to signal his surrender. The three new arrivals wore armored battle suits, designed to take a beating from anything short of a fighter's cannon. Rake nodded as understanding sunk in. *The commandos are in light gear so they could get up to seal us in, but the big guys here were meant to do any real fighting. They must have been using those magnetic cables to zip-line in; otherwise, those suits don't have the mobility to do an insertion this high up.*

Rain lashed in through the broken windows, and water poured off the three men in battle suits. Rake called out again, "We surrender!"

Coilguns chattered again, making themselves heard above the storm. Rake closed his eyes and waited for the bullets to rip the life from his body.

He was wholly disappointed.

An explosion rocked the tower, and Rake opened his eyes in time to see the Terran gunship falling away with smoke and flame billowing from its aft. A moment later, the three battle suited-men were jerked backward, still attached to the magnetic lines, screaming as they were pulled out the window.

Rake dove for his gun, came out of a shoulder-roll with the weapon in hand, and sprayed fire across the doorway.

They're not going to be in any hurry to charge in here with only light armor, he thought to himself. *Not when they were expecting to the battle suits to do all the work.*

"Meg!" he shouted. "The viewport!"

Outside, through the rain, the familiar shape of the *Starfall* was outlined against the clouds. New magnetic lines were already snapping into place through the shattered windows.

The girl didn't hesitate - she ran to the viewport and jumped out, grabbing one of the fastened lines. The *Starfall* dropped a half-dozen meters of altitude, and suddenly she was sliding down the line toward the safety of the starship.

Rake followed, firing blindly behind him as he ran. He stopped at the window just long enough to jam the sidearm in his holster, then jumped.

He nearly missed the line as the *Starfall* jerked, trying to maintain a steady altitude - a mean feat for a starship hovering in atmosphere perhaps a hundred meters over the planet's surface. Rake caught the cable by fingertip and barely held on as it started to slide, generating friction and pain. Fear overrode his body's reflexes, and he snagged the cable more firmly, then got his other hand wrapped tightly around it as he slid down toward the waiting ship.

XII

AREE HERSELF MET RAKE AT THE airlock, her hair wet and wind-whipped from the storm. A fierce grin slashed across her face as she hauled Rake into the *Starfall*. "Welcome aboard, Weston," she said with a warrior's cheer. "Glad you could join us."

"Me, too," Rake said breathlessly. "How did you know?"

"Wirst was listening to communication traffic while he was working on the *Starfall*, and when the radio lit up with Terran naval encryption, he knew enough to grab us and point us in the right direction." Caree's good cheer was infectious. "The Terrans never knew what hit 'em."

"Too bad Shoram didn't make it," Rake mumbled, but the sheer exhilaration at *being alive* was overriding the pain of loss.

"So, where to now?" the captain asked.

"Before the Terrans gunned him down, Shoram told me where he thought I parked my ship," the pilot said. "So, swing back to the starport and drop me off so I can pick up my airskimmer."

"The airskimmer?" Caree frowned. "Why the airskimmer? The *Starfall* is faster, and we really should be off-planet quick with the mess we left behind at Shoram's tower."

"We will be, but if something else goes wrong, I'll need you as backup," Rake explained. He froze for a moment. "We have to go back to the tower."

"Wait, what? Go back?" Caree raised her eyebrows. "Why in the hell would we fly back into that mess?"

"For this," Meg said from the inside hatch of the airlock, holding up a small box.

It was Rake's turn to be surprised. "How did you...?"

"I grabbed it when I was running for the ship, when you were covering me. Figured you'd want it." The girl smiled shakily. "That was okay, wasn't it?"

"You could've gotten yourself killed doing that," the man said with a shake of his head. "But thank you. I'm going to need that."

"Is that...an AI?" Caree asked.

"Yeah. I'm going to need it on the ship," Rake explained briefly. "So, drop me off, but keep your radio live. If something bad happens, I'll let you know to come gunning in to rescue me."

"Us," Meg interrupted.

Rake shrugged. "Okay, us."

"Calling the cavalry twice is going to cost you extra, Weston."

* * *

Rake enjoyed the silence of the airskimmer's cockpit for three minutes before Meg broke down and started talking.

It had been a productive three minutes - strapping into the small skimmer, running through the abbreviated checklist, swearing at the faulty ionic lifter until it accepted power and let the craft lift from the slip where it had been docked.

All of that had been managed in the first sixty seconds. It took the next sixty to clear the traffic around the starport, such as it was, and to finally reach some clear sky where he could lay on some real speed. That left one more minute to get the skimmer cruising through open air toward the not-so-distant Windward Island.

Then Meg apparently couldn't stand the silence any longer. "I have a question for you," she announced.

"That's hardly a surprise."

"Very funny."

"I thought so."

"Are you going to answer my question or not?" the girl asked irritably.

"You haven't asked it yet."

She snorted at the pilot. "Fine. How come you never mention your ship by name? It's always just 'my ship' or 'the ship'. Every pilot and captain I've ever met talks about his ship like it's a person, except you."

"Because I'm not a sentimental idiot," Rake answered cheerfully. "Any other questions?"

The girl snorted again from the skimmer's back seat. "What does *that* mean?"

"It means I'm wondering if you have any other questions," the pilot said in return.

"Not *that*. I mean the part about being a sentimental idiot."

"Oh, that," Rake feigned innocence. "Most people get too attached to their ships. They name their ship and the moniker sticks, and that makes them easier to find when a skiptracer or some lawman comes hunting for them. There's a whole lot of people in the Expanse that don't remember faces, but they remember ships - especially ships with clever names."

"So you don't care about your ship?" Meg asked skeptically.

"I care about it plenty," Rake allowed, "but I don't let myself get too attached. A ship is a tool, nothing more. I've got twenty or thirty IDs in its computer, and I try to make them all as unobtrusive as possible. Keeping a low profile is far more conducive to long life than flashy names and sentimentality."

Meg shook her head. "You're a strange man, Weston."

"Not strange," he contradicted, "just better than any other pilot and smuggler you've ever encountered."

"Well, you're definitely as egotistical as any other pilot or smuggler I've talked to," she retorted.

"It's not bragging if it's true," Rake grinned.

Meg fell back into a sullen silence, and Rake concentrated on flying the airskimmer.

Windward Island, even by airskimmer, was not far from New Ziric - a short enough ride that Meg hadn't started chattering in Rake's ear yet by the time they were over the rocky island. Rake put the airskimmer into a long, easy bank to get a good look down on the island.

Shoram wasn't exaggerating when he said there's nothing here, Rake thought in dismay. The island bore little signs of vegetation - from the airskimmer's altitude, it appeared to be nothing but a large unbroken stone mass. He knew if he'd shed height, the mass would turn into broken hills and valleys.

"How are we going to find your ship?" Meg asked. "That's a lot of rock to search."

"Yeah, it is," Rake agreed. "So, I'll drop you off on one end and you can start walking. I'll set down at the other, and we'll meet in the middle."

"Very funny." The girl shook her head. "What's your plan?"

"I hope I followed my usual procedure," Rake murmured. He tapped the controls, engaging the airskimmer's autopilot before he started fiddling with the radio.

"What are you doing?" Meg asked.

"Finding my ship," Rake growled. "Be quiet." Ignoring the very loud silence in the skimmer's cockpit, he keyed a series of tones into the skimmer's computer - twenty-five in all - and then set them to transmit.

The radio remained silent.

No response. Dammit, I must not have set the computer before I left, he thought with gritted teeth. *Going to make it a lot harder to find my ship.*

He started to key the airskimmer's computer for a topographical scan of the island when the radio gave a single, five-second tone in response. A smile tugged his lips back.

Something finally went right.

"Got a location," he called back to Meg as the skimmer's map pulsed with a transmission location. "We'll be there in a few moments."

Miraculously, the ionic thrusters held when Rake brought the skimmer down as close as he could to the transmission location - near a deep crevice difficult to see from altitude but obvious when his craft was practically on top of it. With little fuss, he set the skimmer down and dialed back the engines.

If this all goes well, I'll radio Wirst on the way out and let him know where I left his toy.

"Stay here," Rake ordered the girl as he slid the canopy back and climbed out of the skimmer.

"What, so you can take off and leave me here?" she asked cynically.

The pilot rolled his eyes. "Have I left you behind yet?" he countered. "I'll answer that for you. No, I haven't. So sit tight while I make sure the ship is clear and ready to fly. There's every chance a half-dozen skiptracers are waiting in New Ziric watching for my ship. When I'm ready to go, I'll come back and get you, and we'll jump out of here together, okay? Besides," he finished, "I need a set of eyes up here in case someone else comes flying in on this pile of rocks."

"Fine," she muttered, thrusting the AI box toward him. "You'll want this, too."

"Thank you," Rake said graciously, taking the box and slipping it under his arm.

He clambered down from the airskimmer, walked over to the edge of the hole in the ground, and looked down. Difficult to see in the shadow, he could just make out the familiar lines of his ship, well concealed twenty meters below ground level. Rake grimaced as he continued to study the hole.

Miserable climb down, he concluded, *and I think this hole is below sea level, which means it's going to be* wet, *too.*

Sighing, he readjusted his grip on the box and slid over the edge of the hole. Operating as much by touch as by sight, he carefully lowered himself step by step down the craggy rock face, well aware that a slip would mean a broken bone at best, with the worst including a broken neck or death.

As he worked his way down to his concealed ship, he reflected back on the brief firefight at Shoram's tower.

Something felt wrong about the encounter, but he couldn't immediately put a finger on it.

It's not surprising the Terran team was still on-planet, he told himself. *A special ops team like that would very likely lay low, especially if they knew I had an insurance policy and could be coming back.*

I doubt Shoram sold me to the Terrans. If he did, it was a really stupid way to do it, since he got himself killed. Granted, he might have had an insurance policy of his own, but there would have to be an easier way to hand me over. So why was that encounter so odd? What's wrong with the picture?

Tumblers began to fall together, and abruptly Rake understood just why it was bothering him.

They tried to kill me outright. Slade tried to take me alive at the insurance facility, and at Lantash they bombed the ring to try to get the smuggler hole there to give me up in one piece. Here, though, they didn't try to get me to surrender - they just raked the whole place with coilguns and then sent in the commandos. If they wanted me alive, that would have been a good way to screw it up.

Rake swallowed hard as he followed his chain of logic.

If they're willing to kill me now, there's only one logical conclusions. The Terrans decided killing me is preferable to taking me alive - which probably means they want to shut me up. If that's the case, my odds of getting out of this alive are worse than I thought. Maybe I'd be safe if I can make it through one of the chokepoints to the other half of the Expanse, but that'd be a gamble in itself.

And then there's still Boss Bruno to consider. The bits and pieces I'm hearing is that this all started with a job I pulled for him, and that he wants my blood, but the only skiptracer I've seen so far claimed he was working for the Terrans, *not Bruno. If he really wants to drag me in, how could his people be missing me so thoroughly? Bruno's got enough cash he's probably got contacts inside the Terran military, so he's got to know I'm on the* Starfall *with Caree and her crew, but no sign of anyone gunning for them yet, either.*

So what am I missing here?

Rake finally set foot on the ship's topside, the smooth metal a welcome relief from the uneven face of the hole.

And I still don't know what I got myself into, and what that last job was. I mean, what could I have done that both the Terrans and Boss Bruno are gunning for me? They sent a damned fleet *to Lantash to try to trap me there, and that's not cheap.*

It's got to be something critical, something that could upset the balance of power in the Expanse. This can't be something as simple as drugs or theft, unless it was a theft of military secrets. It's got to be something big.

So what is it?

He found the topside maintenance hatch, set the AI box aside, and hooked his fingers in the groove, giving a solid heave. As expected, the hatch swung upward neatly with nary a sound in spite of the effort Rake had to expend to open it. The interior of the ship was pitch-dark, as he had expected, so he picked up the AI box and slid down the ladder into the interior of the ship.

The maintenance hatch was just aft of the ship's cockpit, and he wasted no time walking the half-dozen steps around the corner and up into the cockpit.

Amber lights glowed across the status boards, indicating their powered-down state. Rake paid little mind as he set the AI box down again and began feeding power into critical ship systems and running through his pre-flight checklist. "Twenty minutes of preflight and we'll be on our way," he said aloud as the vessel's lights came up, providing much-needed illumination.

"I'm glad you agree," a feminine voice said sharply. Before Rake could react, she prodded him once with the barrel of her gun. "And none of that quick draw stuff," she drawled. "I've heard you're fast, but if you try to spin and shoot me I will riddle you with holes."

"Can I turn?" Rake asked quietly.

"Not yet," the woman said. Her hand slid against Rake's leg and withdrew his sidearm from his holster. "There, now we can be friends."

"Friends, huh?" the pilot grumbled as he slowly turned his chair around.

"No need to be unfriendly yet," she offered.

Rake took a moment to study the woman. She wore a set of light combat armor, similar to the garb favored by Terran commandos, though it was styled with dark purple camouflage patterns. Her eyes and hair were a matched light blue, and her face was striking at first glance. Her visage was unscarred, but the steel in her expression left no doubt she was an old hand. "You're the one holding the gun," he said casually. "Doesn't seem real friendly."

"I'm just doing what I have to, Weston."

"Uh-huh." He studied the woman for another few moments as she studied him in return. "So, are you one of Bruno's thugs?"

She snorted. "Hardly. I'm an independent - that's the only way to work as a skiptracer."

"So who are you planning on selling me to?" Rake asked cautiously.

Maybe I can get some more information about what the hell is going on from her, he thought.

"I really haven't decided," the blue-haired woman confessed. "Both Bruno and the Terrans are offering a lot of money for your head, but then I got word just a few hours ago that the Terrans have switched from a live-capture to corpse. Way I figure it, I'll auction you off - highest bidder decides if they want the live trap or just some remains." She offered a toothy grin. "Nothing personal, of course."

"Yeah, nothing personal," Rake muttered disgustedly. "Just my life."

"Like I said, nothing personal," the skiptracer said. "It's just business, and unfortunately for you, you're my business today."

Rake considered the new information.

Well, she's confirmed Boss Bruno is one of the people who wants my head. Also looks like the Terrans really are *trying to kill me.* "Are there any other parties offering cash for me?" he asked.

"You're full of questions."

148

"Helps pass the time," Rake said, furiously trying to find a way out.

Meg is sitting up top in the airskimmer. Sooner or later she'll figure something's wrong, right? She wouldn't just come climbing down into this hole.

Would she?

"So far, no," the skiptracer admitted. "I'd be glad to find another buyer for you, if I knew why everyone was chasing you in the first place."

"I wish I knew that myself," Rake said. "Nobody has been real inclined to tell me - it's mostly been demands to give myself up, when they weren't just trying to take my head off."

"Pity," the woman said cheerfully. "Unless you've got the cash to buy out your contract from me, I'm afraid it'll be the Terrans or Bruno."

"What's the price on my head, anyway?" the pilot asked.

The skiptracer told him.

"Yeah, I don't have enough credits to buy a damned carrier," he said with a shake of his head. "And a fighter wing to fly off it, for that matter."

"I was leaning more toward three or four smaller ships," she said. "I've always wanted to be a commodore, or maybe an admiral." She gave him another appraising glance. "You're sure you have no idea what you did? I've never seen a bounty this big."

"Really, I have no idea," Rake said with a reluctant shake of his head. "I've been trying to figure it out since I woke up at the insurance facility at Terra." He offered her another appraising look. "You have me at the disadvantage," he commented.

"That's sort of the point."

"Your name," he said. "I don't know your name."

"Gail," the woman said. "Seems only polite."

"I do have a question for you, if you'd answer it," Rake said, a new fear occurring to him. "How did you find me?"

"Find you?" Gail repeated. "I didn't find you. I've been sitting here waiting for you to come back."

"How did you know where my ship was, then?" he persisted.

"Oh. Well, we were both here when you shot yourself, so I was fairly certain you'd come back."

XIII

...SHOT MYSELF," RAKE SAID dumbly.

The skiptracer raised an eyebrow. "You didn't know?"

"How was I supposed to know?" he said, his mouth running while his brain was processing the new information. "It's not like I remember anything after my last brain flash update. There's no way for me to have known how I died."

Gail shrugged, a dismissive gesture. "I didn't know what you left behind for yourself. It didn't take you too long to return, so I figured you knew everything you had before you ate your own gun."

"No, I don't," was all he could manage as his brain raced through the potential ramifications of the new information.

Okay, so I shot myself rather than be taken, and I have Terrans and Boss Bruno after me. Was it something I had, something I did…or something I knew? Instinctively, he knew he was on the right track. *If it were some cargo or other item, killing myself wouldn't have kept it out of their hands. It had to be information of some kind - something crucial, something critical to both the legal and illegal worlds.*

An eerie, irrational worry struck him.

What if it was…no, it couldn't be. It couldn't *be.*

Rake pushed it aside, refused to even consider the possibility.

It would *be critical for everyone, from Terra to the furthest colony world. But it couldn't be.*

Could it? No, it couldn't, so stop thinking about it, Weston.

"So, what's your plan?" Rake asked casually. "Fly my ship out of here, take me to some rock somewhere and keep me tied up until one side or the other delivers the money?"

"Something like that," Gail said. "Except *some rock* will be right here. No need to take you anywhere, and if I move you the odds of something going wrong are far worse."

Rake grudgingly offered a nod of admiration. The woman had clearly thought through her plan, and several days alone on his ship had allowed her adequate time to familiarize herself with its layout and, more than likely, find the various secrets he had layered in its hull for such contingencies.

"Don't resist," she said warningly as she stepped closer. From a pouch on her belt she withdrew a handful of plastic bands. With practiced ease, she one-handedly bound Rake to the pilot's chair, her off hand keeping her own wide-barreled sidearm trained on him the entire time. "Remember," she said, "I want to make the most money off this possible, but if necessary I can just turn your corpse over to the Terrans. Help yourself by helping me."

When the blue-haired woman had finished and she stepped back, Rake had to ask, "What sort of pistol is that? I've never seen one like it."

"They're a new type, called a Dagon," Gail said with a smile, slipping easily into shop talk. "Someone came up with the design on Huaxa - they pack a lot more punch than your standard sidearm. Your pistol here, and most sidearms shoot one bullet at a time. Dagons shoot a burst of smaller bullets, all at the same time. They're not real effective past ten meters or so, but inside that range it'll punch a hole through powered armor and kill the sucker wearing it."

Rake frowned. "Sounds like you wouldn't get more than a couple shots before you'd be out of power."

Gail dug withdrew a cylinder from her belt. "They use these," she explained. "You pack them in advance - a high-charge capacitor on one end, and your shots on the other. On this Dagon, you can load eight of them in the weapon itself and fire until you're empty, and it takes just a few seconds to reload. If you don't use your rounds within a few weeks, you have to recharge the capacitors, but that's simple enough and only takes a few seconds per cartridge."

"So you trade convenience and immediate number of rounds for short-range firepower," Rake commented. "Interesting concept. I might have to look into that." He hesitated a moment before asking, "So, now what? Are you waiting for me to fall asleep or something before you start calling up the Terrans and Boss Bruno and getting your auction started?"

"Hardly. I had the transmission setup and ready to go on my ship days ago - when you dropped in, I just released it." Gail smiled indulgently. "Because it came from my ship at the starport, no one will know where we're sitting - which is important if I'm going to keep the winner from welching on the debt."

"Can't have that," he agreed tightly.

I really am screwed this time. No suiciding out, even if I could get to a gun - no insurance policy waiting for me this time. My only chance is Meg figuring out something is wrong and calling in the cavalry, but she's way more likely to climb down here and get herself shot. Which means, if I want to save her life...

"By the way," he offered, "you might want to know, there's a girl sitting in the airskimmer topside waiting for me. I'd be obliged if you didn't kill her."

"Nice of you to mention that," Gail said appreciatively. "Is there a price on her skin, too?"

"Not as far as I know."

"Good, then I have no reason to shoot her, and we can keep this amicable." Gail narrowed her eyes and leaned down, looking Rake squarely in the eye. "Of course, that depends on what instructions you left her with."

"I told her to stay put until I cleared her to follow me, and alert me if she saw anything suspicious, like a Terran ship searching the island," Rake answered. "Nothing else."

Gail nodded in satisfaction. "You're telling the truth."

"Of course I am."

"She can stay put, then," the skiptracer said. "I can't imagine it will take too long for the Terrans or Bruno to reply."

"Well, if we're going to sit here and wait," Rake said slowly, "can I use the ship's computers?"

Gail laughed, an honest rolling chuckle that continued for nearly a minute, ending with gasps for breath and tears on her cheeks. "Sure, I'm just going to let you use the computer on your own ship. So you can radio for help, or activate whatever traps you have inside here, or maybe fire the engines to draw attention to us. Yeah, I don't think so."

"You could supervise me," he offered. "Just watch over my shoulder. I wouldn't try to hide anything from you."

"Now why would I do that?" the skiptracer asked between guffaws. "Seems like a lot of risk and no reward."

"It might make me far more valuable," Rake said, tossing out some bait. "I mean, you know about the kind of money being offered for me. Wouldn't it be better if you knew just *why* they're offering that kind of cash?"

"No, for two reasons," Gail said firmly. "First, as a skiptracer, it's only professional - I don't ask why, I just collect on the offered rewards. Second, if someone wants to offer that kind of money for you *dead* without you having some heinous crimes on your official record, they'd probably take my head off just for knowing the same information. I like keeping my head attached to my neck, so I'll take a pass on that."

"Wonderful," Rake muttered. "First skiptracer I've ever even *heard* of that wouldn't be interested in some valuable information."

"Oh, don't get me wrong, I'm interested," she contradicted. "Just not interested enough to risk your contract and my life."

They settled into an uneasy silence, the skiptracer sitting on a console and Rake banded to the pilot's chair. Rake worked up various escape plans in his head, but none of them reached the actuation stage due to fundamental flaws - he was bound hand and foot, the skiptracer was armed, he couldn't reach the ship's controls, the engines were shut off, he hadn't installed the new AI yet. Ultimately, it was a frustrating enterprise, but it helped pass the time.

Finally, the skiptracer's personal radio beeped.

"Ah, 'bout time," she said brightly. She held up her gauntlet and showed the flashing light to her bounty. "If you'll excuse me."

"Take your time," Rake mumbled as she retreated as far off the bridge as she could while still keeping an eye on him.

Yeah, she's not going to leave me sitting alone here...and even if she did, it's not like I can just break these bands and walk away.

He leaned back in the chair, felt it conform to his back. Feeling helpless, he looked out of the cockpit and up the hole overhead, where a small wedge of sky was visible.

If I don't find a way out, I'm never going to be flying those skies again. Think, Rake!

And then he saw something utterly unexpected.

The *Starfall* was dropping toward the island.

His heart surged with hope.

We're not out of this yet, he thought fiercely. *Meg must have called for help.*

Just as quickly, his heart fell as a second ship crossed that same bit of sky - at a far higher altitude, and moving so fast he nearly missed it, but utterly identifiable even as a speck in the sky.

"Gail!" he shouted. "Gail! Get over here!"

The skiptracer's booted feet pounded a staccato back to the cockpit. "What is it, Weston?" she asked.

"Who were you talking to, the Terrans or Boss Bruno?" he asked urgently.

"The Terrans," she answered. "They've been reluctant to match Bruno's latest offer, and one of the Terran commanders was giving me the whole amnesty-and-patriotism speech to try to talk me down. Why?"

"We have to go, *now!*" Rake snarled. "There's a Terran gunship overhead."

The skiptracer's blue eyes widened in shock. "Are you sure?"

"Yes. Just caught a glimpse of it before I lost it in the clouds," he said. "You need to cut me out of here, or they're going to turn this hole into our graves!"

Gail did nothing for a long moment, studying the bound man.

She's not sure if I'm telling the truth, Rake realized.

At last, the skiptracer flicked her wrist, and a knife slipped from inside her bracer. "That uniformed monkey was keeping me on the channel to backtrace us," she hissed as she stepped toward Rake. "I bet they found my ship and the relay I setup. I should have guessed they'd try to double-cross me."

Rake looked up nervously as she towered over him with the blade. "So, you're going to sell me to Boss Bruno, aren't you?" he asked.

"Maybe," she allowed as she brought the blade down and cut the first of his bands. "But we're going to need each other for the next few minutes to get out of here alive. Assuming you were telling the truth, of course," she added as she cut the other band holding his wrists, then stepped away.

"Uh, my legs?" Rake prodded.

"Not going to happen. How fast is your preflight?"

"Full preflight takes about twenty minutes, but I can have us in the air in under three," Rake said grimly, rotating the chair around to bring the controls into reach. He felt off-balance with his legs bound to the chair, but he tried to ignore it as he flooded the reactor with fuel and fed power into the engines. "C'mon, baby," he muttered as he worked, "let's get into the skies. Quickly, now."

As the sensors came online, his screens began to light up with data. Gail leaned over his shoulder and grimaced. "We must have cut transmission before the Terrans got a full fix on our location, but with that search pattern he'll find us in five minutes or less."

"Hopefully the hole keeps him from seeing our reactor signature," Rake said. "Engines will be flight capable in just over a minute."

"What do you have for guns on this thing?" she asked.

"Can you fly?" he asked in return.

She eyed him suspiciously. "Why do you ask?"

"Because you can't operate the weapons," he said bluntly. "All the offensives are operated by neurals only, and we don't have time to calibrate you to the ship even if you *do* have the equipment."

The skiptracer brushed her hair back from her neck to reveal a neural interface jack. "Yes, I can fly," she said grimly.

"Good. But you're going to have to cut me loose if we're going to make this work," he warned. "The pilot controls are all here, so unless you want to sit on my lap…"

"Is your preflight done?" Gail asked.

Rake snapped a pair of switches. "Close enough. Fifteen more seconds to warm up the drives and we're ready to fly."

Gail snatched up a cable laying on the console. "This is your weapons interface, right?" she asked. When Rake nodded, she dropped the cable and pulled a pair of ties from her pouch again. With the same practiced ease, she re-bound Rake's hands to the chair.

"Hey, what's this?" he protested.

Without bothering to answer, she picked up the cable again, pulled it over to Rake, and snapped it into his freshly-installed interface.

Sensor data began flooding directly into Rake's mind. He shook his head at the sudden disorientation, and was further distracted when Gail plopped herself down in his lap. She pulled the chair's safety harness over both of them, snugging them tightly in place, before grasping the ship's yoke and throttle.

Rake closed his eyes to better focus on the data flooding his brain, but it was hard to manage with a woman sitting on his lap and literally strapped against him. He wished fleetingly he had time to run through the system calibration - the newly-installed implant wasn't quite identical to his previous equipment, in spite of the shop's repeated assurances - but Rake suspected Gail wouldn't allow it even if they didn't have an armed Terran ship overhead.

The ship's engines whined with effort as the craft slowly lifted out of the hole. Unpleasant scrapes drew complaints from the ship's computer, and the resulting damage reports flooding the neural interface felt physically painful.

Miscalibration or not, it feels like I'm wearing *this ship*, Rake noted distantly. *Or maybe it's like my own skin. Either way, this is terrible.*

When they breached the edge of the hole, the sensors reported another ship nearby: the *Starfall*, resting on its skids with airlock open. The Terran gunship was clearly visible, too - its active sensors, searching for Rake and Gail, likely was lighting up every passive sensor within five hundred kilometers.

And it was dropping like a stone toward the two outlaw vessels.

Rake concentrated on swinging his ship's guns around, but they felt sluggish to his commands. Dimly, he felt his fists tighten and loosen, and he ached to hold the physical controls. It wasn't an option, though, so he focused his thoughts on the guns and the sensor data, trying to merge the two into a single purpose. The visuals, usually so crisp and clear, were blurry and out-of-focus, and he had a hard time comprehending the data.

The gunship was juking now as it dropped, rocking back and forth to foul targeting. If his interface had been working normally, the primitive maneuvers wouldn't have been enough - not without a good electronics countermeasure broadcast, which the Terran warship was neglecting to employ, presumably to allow its crew to use their own computerized targeting to the best of its capability. But with Rake struggling to use the neurals, he couldn't get a good enough bead on the ship to even try firing.

Belatedly, he realized it was the same gunship that had attacked Shoram's tower - much of its juking was actually due to damaged control surfaces and a misfiring engine. The crew had apparently managed to get it airborne, but full repairs would have taken longer than the brief hours that had passed.

Gail's cursing didn't help as she struggled with the ship's controls. The vessel was rocking unsteadily as its keel cleared the hole, and the skiptracer was having trouble transitioning the ship from upward thrust to forward motion.

"She has enough power that you can run the mains up to thirty percent before you have to start pulling from the lifters," Rake advised between clenched teeth as he fought to lock the guns onto the still-falling Terran gunship. "She's too heavy in atmo to run the lifters at anything less than a hundred percent during takeoff until you've got at least the mains up to fifteen."

"Just shoot," Gail growled in his ear. "Let me fly."

"I would, but you're not flying. This is barely keeping her from falling."

"Shut up and shoot," she repeated, but the ship stabilized as she followed his advice.

Rake still didn't have a reliable shot at the Terrans, but he opened fire anyway. White tracers flashed up through the air from the coilguns, bright streaks visible even in the bright sunlit skies. *Give 'em something else to think about*, he thought.

The Terran military ship abruptly heeled over and dove even faster. Smoke trailed from its drives, and Rake thought for a brief moment that he had somehow tagged the gunship in spite of its maneuvers and his poor neural connection. Belatedly, though, he realized the *Starfall* was shooting as well.

The gunship suddenly leveled out as though it had hit a glass floor, a stop so abrupt that Rake wondered if the crew could survive such a maneuver. It hung in the air like a cloud, unmoving for a long second and a half, and Rake fired again.

I could be shooting without a neural connection at all and make this shot connect.

Fire erupted from the Terran vessel's hull, and it began to fall again - completely uncontrolled now, tumbling without any sort of pattern. Rake followed its descent until it crashed spectacularly into the ocean, sending a plume of water hundreds of meters into the air.

Then his ship rocked from a nearby explosion. Gail was swearing again and fighting to keep it in the air, but Rake could do nothing but watch.

What? What was that?

He looked around frantically with the sensors, trying to locate the second attacker.

There wasn't one.

The *Starfall* had exploded.

XIV

P UT THE SHIP DOWN," RAKE demanded.

"Not happening," Gail said coolly. "There's every chance the Terrans have more ships coming, and I'm not sticking around here to find out."

"Put the ship down," he insisted. "Those are my friends down there, and *they're* the ones who shot the gunship down, not me. Put us down, *now!*"

The skiptracer said nothing as she slid the ship over and dropped it down to a rough landing on the skids. Rake grimaced as the vessel bounced before coming to rest, trying to ignore the likely damage to his vessel.

When they were securely on the ground, Gail unstrapped from the pilot's chair and slid off Rake's lap, then flashed her knife at him before slashing open the ties.

"Go," she grunted. "But remember that if you do anything stupid, I *will* shoot you."

"We'll talk about that in a minute," Rake said with a nod as he rose to his feet, jerking the neural link out before sprinting aft to the airlock.

What remained of the *Starfall* was a burning scrap heap by the time his feet were on the dirt. He grimaced as he watched, well aware that he was probably getting a healthy dose of radiation from the destroyed vessel's no-doubt breached fuel tanks.

I'm going to need to go through full decon, he thought wearily as he looked around. *Did Meg at least survive?*

The airskimmer had been kicked end-over-end by the *Starfall*'s detonation. Wasting no time, Rake ran over the rocky island to the twisted shell of the airskimmer and looked inside.

He was shocked to find not only Meg - unconscious, bleeding, and still alive - but Caree in the pilot's seat!

A likely scenario played out in his head.

Meg started worrying when I didn't return. She signaled the Starfall, *which arrived right before the Terran gunship. Caree left the ship to talk to Meg, and they were sitting in the airskimmer trying to figure out what to do when the gunship started attacking. The* Starfall*'s crew reacted to defend themselves and their captain, and died fighting.*

He checked Caree's pulse, found it still strong in spite of the trauma. Making a snap decision, he crawled into the airskimmer and unclipped Meg's flight harness. He wasn't a particularly large man, and it took a good deal of sweating and swearing to extract the girl from the skimmer - and a lot more work to carry her back to his ship.

In spite of his bravado to the skiptracer, Rake was sweating as much with nervousness as exertion when he finally laid Meg onto one of the beds in the medical bay. One more quick check to ensure she was still breathing, and then he was out the airlock again to recover Caree.

As he stumbled back to his ship with the *Starfall*'s captain in his arms, he wondered very briefly how she would react when she awoke. Her vessel and crew were dead, caught on the ground by the Terrans - and she had failed to go down with the ship. If she were like other small ship captains, her entire fortune was tied up in the vessel; she was likely now destitute.

It was an ugly thought, and Rake resolved to consider it only after Caree awoke.

When he had both women laid out in the tiny room, he activated the medical AI and stepped back to allow it to work.

Articulating arms descended from the bay's ceiling, complicated contraptions with a variety of tools built in - sensors tuned for detection and monitoring of human life markers, laser and physical cutting instruments, needles with lines snaking back to storage capsules with dozens of medications, and a dozen other tools that Rake couldn't even identify.

He knew of no spacer who preferred such treatment - living doctors were always better than an unsupervised AI - but he didn't have the necessary skills to repair whatever injuries they had taken in the blast, and he had personally trusted the AI before to save his own life.

It would have to be enough.

Still need to decon, he told himself. *But first, we need to get into the air.*

He walked forward, most of the urgency gone - though the possibility of another Terran ship lurking around was not trivial - and found Gail still in the cockpit, watching the sensors as though they were mere entertainment.

"Let's go," he said wearily.

Gail laughed, a short and bitter sound. "Go where? The Terrans want you dead, and badly. They spiked my ship over at the starport - now it's a flaming wreck. Even if I wanted to turn you over to Boss Bruno, I doubt we'd survive the trip there - not with the Terrans looking for you. I'd bet every resource I have stashed away that they're waiting for us along the trade routes. And after this, there's no way I'd sell you to them - not after they tried to kill me, too. That's bad business."

"If we keep sitting here, we definitely won't survive the trip, because we won't be moving. Hence, no trip," Rake said. "Get us on a course for Earth."

The skiptracer frowned at him. "Earth? The planet's hardly anything but ash, and it's right next door to Terra. Why would we go to Earth?"

"Because it's our way out of this mess," Rake said grimly. "It's the only lead I have left on just what I got myself into."

The woman shrugged, a ripple running through the cascade of blue hair from the motion. "Fine, Earth it is."

"I'm going to hop through decon," he told the skiptracer. "Let me know if anything else goes wrong."

"I'm sure something will."

* * *

Decontamination chambers were almost universally employed across starships. They served a single purpose - to ensure that a subject was clean of any alien diseases or radiation. Though every world humanity had settled had been terraformed before settlers had set foot outside transport ships, there were always unique diseases and life that sprung up from the territories, often just as virulent as anything from Earth.

They were also almost universally hated.

Full decontamination took time, and due to the nature of decon, a subject couldn't take anything with him into the chamber - not a book, or a simple computer pad, or clothes. Further, there was nothing to do in the chamber but sit and wait.

Radiation decon, which Rake needed, was a relatively quick procedure - two hours, and he would be scoured clean. While Caree and Meg alike would both be undergoing a similar decon procedure in the medical bay, they were fortunate enough to be sleeping through it.

Rake, on the other hand, doubted he'd be sleeping for some time.

While the decon procedure began - largely invisible to him, save a digital readout on the wall counting down the seconds until he was free again - the pilot found he had nothing to do but consider the events since he had awoken on Terra.

So, back to the beginning, he reviewed. *As much as I know. Several weeks ago - three weeks now? I took a job from Boss Bruno. Within two weeks of me taking that job, I committed suicide to prevent a skiptracer from apprehending me.*

Between those two events, I know I went to Earth, according to my own navicomputer, and eventually I fled to Clarion, where I died.

When I first woke up on Terra, the skiptracer Slade was waiting for me. He claimed he was working for the Terrans when he nabbed me and started dragging me off the station when Caree and the Starfall *intervened. We fled to Lantash, where the local authorities were waiting for us. We gave them the slip, made it to the smuggler hole in the ring of Lantash Six, and then had to flee again when the Terran fleet arrived.*

We made it to Clarion, where I had left my ship. The Terrans had a team on-world and killed Shoram and tried *to kill me, which suggests a change from the skiptracer trying to take me alive. And then they betrayed the skiptracer who had me at gunpoint, this Gail, in an attempt to kill all of us.*

He leaned against the wall and closed his eyes, trying not to wince at the cold metal against his exposed back.

They've been getting desperate, he realized. *They're afraid I'm closing in on...whatever it is I was doing for Boss Bruno. That's why they tried killing a skiptracer who was negotiating in good faith with them - they didn't want to risk me slipping away again.*

But where is Oscar Bruno in all this? If I had finished his job, the Terrans would probably be chasing him, not me. But I haven't seen any of his goons on my wake, and I can't imagine they're that much slower than the Terrans.

Are they?

Just doesn't seem plausible.

So, all this, and it still doesn't answer the what and the why. Terrans chasing me, bounties on my head, all kinds of destruction, and an entire Terran fleet...and I still don't know why.

He regretted for a moment not breaking protocol and bringing a pad with him into the decon chamber. He ached to rifle through his ship's databanks, even though he was certain they were already wiped clean.

You can't tell me Gail didn't already look, and if she knew the truth, she probably would've been ready for the Terrans to turn on her.

Rake couldn't seem to get comfortable, and opted to lie down flat on the floor instead. When he had finished stretching out prone, he realized how tired he actually was.

Other than some sleep with Caree - and there wasn't much sleep involved there - I don't think I've really rested since I left the Terra insurance facility.

Weariness washed over him, and his eyelids dropped heavier with every passing minute.

I still need to search for any traces I have left in the computer, but if it's anything like my navigational logs, I eliminated it all before I shot myself.

My only lead right now is Earth - well, unless I want to go try to talk to Boss Bruno. And if I stiffed him on a job, I won't survive the conversation.

Of course, even after the Great War, Earth is a big place. This is going to be like searching for the old needle in the haystack, and I don't even have a magnet.

* * *

Ten hours later, freshly bathed and feeling remarkably rested, Rake was hard at work on the ship's bridge, hooking up the new pilot AI.

"I'm not sure why you're bothering with that," Gail commented idly. They were between jumps, the point-to-point drive cooling off as they made a cross-system jaunt to save fuel.

"I've seen the way you fly," Rake said dryly. "If we get into another firefight with Terran warships, I'd rather have a combat AI flying than you. And you can't man the guns without calibrating the neurals, and I really don't want you hooking up your brain to my ship."

"Why not?" the skiptracer asked.

Rake snorted. "Because it's *my ship*," he said coolly.

"Interesting name for a ship," she said casually, her chair swiveled to watch the stars. "The *Mirage*. Very poetic."

The pilot's head snapped around to look at her. "Where did you find that name?" he asked tightly.

"I had several days of just hanging around here," she said with a dismissive wave of her hand, not bothering to turn. "I swept every bit of data I could find. You really need to use better encryption, too - most of it unlocked with old Terran keys from the Great War, and the rest of it was so derivative it took less than half a day to crack it."

The pilot nodded slightly, a show of respect, before turning back to connecting up the pilot AI. "And what did you find?"

"For someone with such poor encryption, you did a great job covering your trail," the skiptracer complained. "Every data recovery tool I've got came up clean on your databanks, and there was nothing useful in your encrypted files. I mean, I can guess *exactly* where this ship came from, but it's like she's straight out of the shipyard with nothing useful added."

"Well, I guess you saved me a few hours of work," Rake grunted as he snapped the last data relay into place. "I don't need to bother digging through the computer if you already did it for me."

"I wouldn't say I was doing it for you," the skiptracer said dryly. "I was looking for anything worth some cash. Not much to be had, though."

"Wonderful," Rake mumbled as he hooked up the power connection. "Sorry for the inconvenience."

"Likewise," the skiptracer said.

"So what's your plan?" the pilot asked. "I mean, when you had me at gunpoint on Clarion, it was pretty clear - sell me to Boss Bruno or the Terrans, whichever paid more.

Now that the Terrans have blown that plan to hell, why are you still here?"

"I'm still looking for a way to make a profit off this," she said with a grim smile. "I mean, sooner or later there's going to be an opportunity for it."

Rake started the AI's power sequence, and a number of lights burned red in a neat line across the box. After a few seconds, the first turned green. "So, does that mean I should be looking for a chance to throw you out the airlock? I'm likely your best chance at a profit."

"Maybe," the skiptracer allowed. "You don't seem like the murderous type, either."

"Can't say I am," Rake admitted. "Doesn't mean I haven't killed plenty."

"Most of us out here have," Gail said casually. "And that's part of *my* business."

The AI's initialization was moving along rather quickly; half the lights had already turned green. "So, you're saying I can trust you."

"You can trust me to look out for my best interests," she corrected. "Which, right now, doesn't include anything that benefits the Terrans. Whether I stick with you or sell you out depends entirely on circumstance."

"Well, I'm sure I'll know it when your gun is in my back," Rake said cheerfully.

"I'll give you warning before I shoot," she said. "It only seems fair, given the circumstances."

The last red light turned green. "I appreciate it. Alright, here we go - initializing the new pilot AI."

"Have you ever done that before?" the skiptracer asked.

"Never had a reason to," he replied. "This should be pretty simple. Just initialize it, give it a name, and let it run through the system checks. If I hooked up all the connections right, it should be ready to fly in a few minutes."

"Wonderful," she said, staring out at the stars. "So, tell me, Weston, what will it profit me to keep your secrets?"

"Excuse me?" Rake asked with a raised eyebrow, turning away from the AI.

"I told you, I had plenty of time to scour the databanks. This is hardly a civilian freighter, any more than you're a civilian."

Rake shook his head. "The Great War's long since done."

"There's no doubt about that, but there are still plenty of open bounties that you might fit neatly into." She frowned thoughtfully. "Though I have to say, I never saw a ship like the *Mirage* before."

"That's because there aren't any," Rake said tightly. "She was one of the prototypes, and the shipyard where her keel was laid down has long since been shut down. After Earth burned and the fleets disappeared, there wasn't much need for warship development."

The AI beeped for his attention. Rake turned to look at it when Gail asked, "What model of AI is that, anyway?"

"Cee-Six," Rake answered.

A computerized voice, distinctly male, emanated from the AI box. "Designation 'Seasick' accepted."

"Wait, what?" Rake frowned at the box.

"I think you just named your new AI," Gail said dryly.

Rake growled at the box. "Wonderful. Just wonderful." He scratched his chin as he looked at the AI. "I thought these things offered a gender selection on voice," he commented.

"Civilian AIs do, but that's a military model," Gail answered. "They're all male-mannerism - probably because they're designed for warships."

Rake gave up a long-suffering sigh. "Well, Seasick you'll be then," he muttered.

"You still haven't answered my question, Captain," Gail commented. "Like I said, there's a lot of bounties out there for Terran officers who served during the war - after all, the survivors of Earth are *still* looking for blood, and you're hardly protected by the rest of the Terran navy like your old comrades, are you?" She snorted. "If I were to guess, I'd bet I could get money for you from the Terrans for turning over a deserter, too."

"You're assuming the Terrans don't shoot you dead after Clarion," Rake shot back.

"True, but the Earth expatriates won't really care about that, now will they?"

"Did you have a reason for bringing this all up?" Rake half-snarled.

"Simple. I want in."

The pilot blinked. "Want in?" he repeated.

"You can't tell me there's no money involved in this," Gail declared. "I want my fair share of the profit from this."

"I don't know there *is* money in this," Rake shot back.

"Of *course* there's money. You think you were doing this job for Boss Bruno for free?"

A thought occurred to Rake. "Question - what've you been hearing from the skiptracer networks about Boss Bruno and me? I mean, I keep hearing I worked for him and screwed up a job, but he's hardly the kind to live and let live. Why haven't I seen any of his usual thugs show up yet?"

Gail shook her head. "Word went out he was looking for you before you ate your gun, but after you were reported dead there hasn't been *anything* from him. No confirmation or withdrawal of the bounty, nothing." She snorted. "If I didn't know better, I'd say you were Bruno and didn't remember it."

"Yeah, not likely."

Gail's back was still turned as she studied the stars. The AI's lights blinked green in rapid succession, indicating an all-pass on the initial system checks. The only thing left now was a flight check, and Rake wasn't in a hurry to do that yet - not until he wasn't fleeing for his life, and could afford to slow down long enough to experiment. *When we reach Earth*, he told himself.

"So why desert?" the skiptracer asked after a lengthy silence.

Rake sat down in the gunner's chair, just behind the pilot seat, and began initializing the neural interface. While he didn't want to risk wasting time with shutting down the engines to run through the pilot AI's trials, recalibrating the neural connection would take little time. "Why do you want to know?" he asked.

"Because I'm still trying to figure out what sort of man you are," Gail answered. "You have an odd sense of loyalty - even with the Terrans on your tail, you insisted on going back to get that girl and the other ship's captain. You also keep cool under fire - most bounties I've hunted aren't going to stand there and banter with me when I've got a gun trained on 'em." She shook her head. "You don't fit the profile of a deserter."

Rake shrugged uncomfortably. "We burned Earth," he said. "Well, not just Earth - the other colonies in the home system were all destroyed or damaged, too. That wasn't a military act, and it wasn't a military target. We killed billions of people, and destroyed our race's home, with just one act."

"It brought the war to an end that much sooner," Gail noted.

"No, it didn't," Rake replied. "What brought the war to an end was the disappearance of both fleets."

The skiptracer sounded skeptical. "I've never bought into that. Fleets of starships don't just disappear."

"They did," Rake said grimly. "This time, at least."

"How do you know?"

"Because I was there."

XV

YOU WERE THERE," GAIL repeated.

Rake nodded. "I was there. Captaining this ship, in fact."

"Then how are you here and not missing like all the other ships in both fleets?" she asked skeptically.

The pilot studied the neural connection as though he hadn't seen it before. "The day after we torched the system, the entire fleet was ordered to jump to Earth to offer aid," he said quietly. "I think the brilliant idea from our High Command was to help pick up the pieces - to show we had won, but we would be gracious."

"Hard to think they'd welcome you with open arms," the skiptracer commented. "You'd just killed most of the system." She frowned. "How did you manage that, anyway? I always assumed the Terrans had firebombed the three colonies and Earth itself, but you're telling me it wasn't there."

"It was far worse than that," he whispered. "All it took was one ship, armed with the Catalyst."

"Catalyst?" she repeated.

"Don't ask me how it worked, because I don't know, but it was supposed to be the new deterrent - the weapon that would make peace possible. Don't cooperate with the Terrans, and we launch it into your system's star, make it burn hotter, and it kills everyone in the system. Even better, it only lasts a day or so, so afterward we can move ships back in and occupy your worlds, send our own colonists, pick up whatever pieces we want." His smile was bitter. "Assuming it hadn't burned up, of course."

"How could someone use a weapon like that?" the skiptracer managed, clearly appalled. "They had to know it would kill billions on Earth alone!"

"Because the Great War had been fought for *years* and nothing changed," Rake said sharply. "Hundreds of thousands of soldiers on both sides died and the battle lines hardly moved. The insurance companies wouldn't contract with the military, so all the troops dying were dead for good." He shook his head. "Honestly, when word filtered down that we were using the Catalyst, most of the people in the service I knew were damned excited that we were finally going to beat back the Earth tyrants."

"So you came in to clean up in the aftermath," Gail said.

Rake nodded. "This little gunship was my first command. It was a prototype design, with two others under construction. We were desperate for any edge we could find, and this was one - a gunship that could be crewed by two or three men, instead of the ten to fifteen most ships this size required."

"So you could field more of them with less crew."

"Exactly," the pilot said. "If we could make the automation and neural connections work well with the gunship, it could have led to a revolution with larger ships, too. Less men, more ships."

"So what happened when you reached Earth?" Gail asked.

"I think events were moving too fast for High Command to gather proper intelligence," Rake said ruefully. "And they all wanted to be present for the official surrender of Earth's forces. When the Catalyst was deployed, they ordered all fleet vessels to return to Terra, and after a day they ordered the entire fleet to jump to Earth."

"And?" she prompted.

"Earth had apparently recalled its fleets, too. Nearly every combat-ready starship in the Expanse was sitting around Earth at the same time."

"And there was a battle," Gail reasoned.

"No, there wasn't." Rake shook his head. "Earth's navy pulled back from the planet and jumped - just gone."

"Where did they go?"

"Wish I knew," the pilot said with a shake of his head. "We were part of a small contingent left behind as a rearguard, and the rest of the Terran fleet jumped out after them."

"There's only a few places they could've gone," Gail said. "And none of them saw the fleets?"

"No. They were just _gone_. Like that, in an instant, and two fleets vanish with nothing to show for it."

"So what did you do?" Gail asked, clearly intrigued.

"The entire rearguard stayed near Earth for two days, and we helped the survivors as best we could. There were maybe a dozen ships and twice that many fighters, so there wasn't a lot we could do. After those two days had passed, the highest-ranking officer in our little rearguard ordered a retreat to Terra."

"And then?"

Rake sighed. "The two other men on the _Mirage_ both decided they were going to desert and stay on Earth - try to help with the cleanup. I wasn't willing to go back to Terra and tell whoever took over High Command that there were two deserters back on Earth; they'd be executed for it. So we said our goodbyes, and I took the _Mirage_ and headed out to find work."

Gail swiveled the pilot's chair around to study Rake. "Do you think that's what this is all about?"

"What? The fleets?" Rake asked skeptically. "Boss Bruno commissioned this job. What good would fleets of warships with dead crews be to him?"

The skiptracer shook her head. "Seems to me that he might be interested in the Catalyst."

The pilot grimaced. "I was afraid you were going to say that."

Gail raised an eyebrow. "You've been thinking about this, haven't you?" It was a statement, not a question.

"Since I found out it started with a job from Bruno, and I knew I had been to Earth," he said grimly. "It would explain why the Terran military has been chasing me around, too - if the Catalyst weapon is still out there, they'd want to get their hands on it."

"Why wouldn't they have built more? They've had enough time since the Great War ended."

"Maybe they have, and they're trying to keep a monopoly on it," Rake suggested. "Would *you* be comfortable with anyone on our end of space having a weapon like that?"

"Hell no," she said emphatically. "If you're right, though, does that mean you found the Catalyst, or at least the lost fleets?"

"Maybe," he allowed. "It's also possible I never got close to them, but the Terrans and Bruno all think I did."

"You're pretty obviously dead set against Bruno having the Catalyst - something I agree with - so why would you have taken the job in the first place?"

Rake paused for a moment as he considered the question. "I wouldn't have. I'd guess he wrapped it up in something else, something innocuous - and when I figured it out, I ran."

"Wonderful. You couldn't have left clues behind for yourself?" she asked irritably. "I mean, you could've made this way easier on us."

"I somehow doubt I thought I'd be shooting myself," Rake said dryly. "I'm also pretty sure I didn't think I'd be running around with Terrans gunning for my head, and that I'd be working with a skiptracer to get myself clear."

"Which means I'm screwed," Gail commented.

"What do you mean?"

"I can't sell you to *either* side," she complained. "The Terrans will probably try to kill me, and there's no way I want Oscar Bruno to have a weapon like that. So now I'm out a lot of cash *and my ship*, with nothing to show for it." She glanced around the cockpit, her eyes moving slower and seeming to soak in detail. "Of course, I could always just take your ship. It would at least cut my losses."

"You really want to fly a prototype ship with no owner's manual?" Rake strived to keep his voice even, in spite of the urge to shoot the skiptracer immediately for even *considering* stealing his ship. "This thing is unique from the chassis up, which means maintenance is a nightmare. You're not going to pull this into a spacedock at Terra and have the mechanics patch it up for you."

"Of course, that's assuming you're right about all this," Gail reasoned. "Maybe Boss Bruno *isn't* after the Catalyst. If he's not, there's no reason I can't sell you to him."

"Pleasant thought," Rake grumbled, studying the neural connection again before setting it down. Instead of continuing with the calibration, he rose from the gunner's chair and headed aft.

"Where are you going?" Gail called from the chair.

"Not far," he said wryly. "It's a small ship."

* * *

Caree and Meg were both awake and sitting up when Rake slid the door open into the medical bay.

"Rake!" Caree said with some surprise in her voice. "Where are we, and where's my ship?"

"You're on my ship," Rake said, steeling himself before adding, "Your ship was destroyed on Clarion."

"*What?!* The *Starfall* is gone?"

The pilot nodded slightly. "She took a salvo from that Terran gunship. It's gone."

Shock rode freely on the woman's face, and her crystal blue eyes welled with tears. "My crew?"

"They were all on the *Starfall*, best I know," Rake said softly. "I'm sorry, Caree."

"Bastard Terrans," she muttered as a pair of tears traced down her cheeks.

"If it helps, we shot them down," he offered. "Left them and their ship at the bottom of Clarion's ocean."

"It doesn't," the dark-haired woman said flatly, "but thank you."

"Where are we?" Meg asked softly, clearly not wanting to disturb the older woman.

"On my ship, en route for Earth," Rake answered.

"Wouldn't it make more sense to ditch the ship?" Meg asked. "Find some hole to crawl into, change your name, and keep your head down. The Expanse is a big place - there has to be enough room to hide from Boss Bruno and the Terrans."

"Maybe," Rake allowed, "but with all the resources they've already thrown at me - remember the fleet at Lantash? - I can't imagine they're going to let me walk away from this, no matter how hard I try to hide. If I'm going to get out of this alive, I need to know what I knew before I died, and use that knowledge to get myself clear. Somehow."

"And how do you do that?" was her question. "Knowing all that didn't help you the first time around, did it?"

The pilot grimaced in return. "Like I said, they're not going to let me slip away quietly, so I'm short on choices. Maybe I can see something I didn't see then. The other option is to let one side or the other catch up with me, and I'm not going to sit in a Terran hotbox or let Bruno's thugs get their hands on me."

"Where are we going?" Caree asked quietly, having spent time composing herself.

"Earth," Rake repeated.

"Why Earth?" the woman asked, confusion evident in her tone. "There's nothing really left there, unless you're going to go sifting through the debris."

"Because it's the only lead I have left," he confessed. "I know I was there before I fled to Clarion and died. Maybe it was just a simple stop on my way to Clarion, but I doubt it."

"Why?" Meg asked.

"Because I told Wirst to wipe the flight computer of any navigation information before Earth," Rake explained. "Wherever I was before that, it had to be at least through the home system." He took a deep breath. "I might have known how screwed I was by the time I made it to Clarion, too. Leaving Earth on the flight computer could have been a hint to myself." He offered a helpless shrug. "If it wasn't, I still don't have anything else to go on."

"How long until we reach Earth?" Meg asked.

"Three jumps, but they'll be quick. Six hours, give or take." He offered a small smile. "I'd recommend everyone get some more rest. The Terrans will catch up with us sooner or later, and Boss Bruno must still have something up his sleeve."

"No chance I can get off?" the blonde girl asked. "You can't drop me anywhere?"

Rake shook his head firmly. "No stops until Earth," he declared. "If we slow down at all, the odds of someone catching up to us are too great. If that happens, I'm dead, and very likely all of you with me. Sticking with me is the better alternative for now."

"Why?" Meg challenged. "Because of the bounty on *your* head? Last I checked, neither Caree nor I had a bounty out for us."

"The Terrans have changed my bounty to a kill order, and they tried backblading the skiptracer who had caught me," Rake retorted. "I think they'd be more than willing to take either or both of you if it would help them grab me."

"Wait, a skiptracer caught you?" Caree asked. "When was this?"

"Oh. Uh, she's in the cockpit. She was waiting on the ship when Meg and I found it." He smiled, a little embarrassed. "She got the jump on me, held me at gunpoint while she was negotiating with the Terrans and Bruno. The Terrans traced her radio and tried to kill us all."

"So that's why you took so long," Meg muttered. "And I thought you were just going to ditch me."

"The idea occurred to me after I went deaf listening to you," the pilot said with a smirk, "but I doubted vacuum would protect me."

Caree laid back on her bed, closing her eyes. "Dammit, Weston, you owe me for this. Everything I had was tied up in that ship, and now it's a pile of scrap metal. There had better be money in this somewhere."

"You're not the first one to demand money from me on this trip," he said sourly.

"Then you'd better come up with a *lot* of money," she commented. "I'm having a hard time feeling sorry for you right now."

"I can see that." He sighed and shook his head. "Get some rest. We'll be coming up on Earth soon, and if it's anything like Lantash or Clarion, the hunters will be biting at our heels before too long."

* * *

Gail was still awake when Rake returned to the cockpit. "Don't you sleep?" he asked her as he sat down in the gunner's chair again.

She didn't turn from staring out at the stars. "No. Why would I sleep?"

"How do you function if you don't sleep?" he asked.

The skiptracer pulled a small vial from a pocket and held it up. "Stims. I can keep myself going for two weeks or so before I need to sleep. Twenty-four hours after that, I'm good for another two weeks."

"That can't *possibly* be good for you," Rake commented.

"Maybe not, but falling asleep on the job could get me dead," she replied cheerfully. "So, how's your harem?"

The pilot stopped and replayed the last statement in his head to ensure he'd heard correctly before saying, "What?"

"Way I figure it, you've been on the outer worlds for a while now, and you went native, right? Taken a couple of lovers for yourself? Definitely makes extended travel more enjoyable, right?"

Rake coughed into his hand. "No, I haven't gone native. I'm usually flying around the Expanse by myself."

"So what's the story there?"

"The brunette was the captain of the *Starfall*, the ship the Terrans blew up on Clarion while coming after *you*," he said, emphasizing the last word. "The blonde was a barkeep on the ring of Lantash before the Terrans came in and started dropping nukes. She kind of wound up on the

Starfall in the confusion, and I haven't been able to ditch her since."

"I can help you with that," the skiptracer offered. "Couple of shots, toss 'em both out the airlock. I'd do this job cheap, given they're already here."

Rake stared at the blue-haired woman. "You're a bit bloodthirsty."

"If I were bloodthirsty, I'd do it for free," she said cheerfully. "I'm just looking to make some extra coin. I'm going to need it to replace my ship." Gail offered him a thoughtful frown. "Speaking of which, you're hard on ships. You're responsible for losing both the *Starfall* and my ship, the *New Dawn*. I'm surprised this crate hasn't blown up underneath us."

"Very funny," Rake growled as he snapped the neural line into place. He keyed for calibration and began walking through the process - slightly tedious, but it wouldn't take long and he wanted to be sure his ship was combat-ready when they hit Earth.

"So, you're telling me you're *not* attached to either of those women back in the medical bay?" Gail asked idly, her back still turned.

"Yes," Rake growled. "For the last time, yes. I haven't gone native on some outer world, and I certainly don't have a string of wives or concubines or whatever following me around."

"Good," Gail said approvingly. "Wanna?"

Rake nearly jerked out the neural interface cable, his head turned around so fast. "You're joking, right?"

"Why would I joke?" she asked innocently. "We've got hours to go, and we could both relax. It would be nice to not be so damned tense when we hit Earth. Besides, for all we know we're going to die there."

"Are you *really* using the 'Sleep with me tonight because tomorrow we may die' line?" the pilot asked, fighting the surreal sense of the entire conversation.

"If it works, absolutely," Gail replied.

"No," Rake replied immediately. "Just...no."

"Why not?"

"Why not? Why not?" His mind spun for a moment before it began to gain traction. "You're a skiptracer who was hunting me for the reward. What happens if I doze off? Would be easy enough for you to strip all my account cards, or shoot me and call the Terrans, or bind me up and call Bruno. No."

"I could do any of that while you're asleep," she pointed out. "For that matter, I could have done it while you were in the decon chamber fully awake. And I didn't. So, that's no reason."

"No," Rake repeated. "Just...no."

"Your loss," the skiptracer commented, leaning back in the seat and plopping her booted feet down on the console. "Such a shame."

The pilot could only shake his head as he studied the top of her head, the only part of her visible over the back of the chair. "You are a strange, strange woman."

"Not strange," Gail replied. "To be a good skiptracer, you need to act decisively and always pursue what you want. Hesitation is what gets tracers killed and people like you caught. It's easier to be certain in the hunt if you live your whole life like that."

Rake just shook his head and concentrated on the neural calibration. "Let me know when we reach Earth."

XVI

EARTH WAS EVERY BIT AS destroyed as Rake remembered it from his previous trip there, right at the end of the Great War.

Well, I was clearly here after that, but it's hard to remember that since I died. Life insurance policies are great, but there's still some downsides.

The *Mirage*'s cockpit felt far too cramped. The vessel was designed to have a crew of only two in the small space - the pilot and the gunner. Now all four of them occupied the narrow chamber, staring down at the blue-and-brown wasteland.

Earth was still technically inhabitable, but few people were returning from the colonies to repopulate the ravaged world. The destruction caused by its own star had ranged from wildfires consuming vast acres of forest and jungle to city-wide infernos that had turned popular cities into ash-filled cairns.

The attack had happened during the summer months in the northern hemisphere, meaning the traditionally stronger nations - the remains of the United States, the ancient Soviet Block, Old Europe, China - had been dealt the brunt of the blow. The weaker nations south of the equator had suffered less damage, but also lacked the extensive infrastructure to quickly deal with the disaster as it unfolded.

Of the estimated ten billion citizens living on the homeworld when the Catalyst had been deployed, less than a hundred million remained. The initial death toll had numbered in the billions, but many more had died in the aftermath due to the breakdown in infrastructure, primarily the distribution networks for both food and water, and vast disease outbreaks due in part to the time it took to properly dispose of the dead.

A majority of the survivors evacuated the badly-damaged world, exacerbating the already-impossible task of maintaining and rebuilding the necessities of modern civilization. With millions of survivors scattering across the Expanse, Earth was sent into a downward spiral, until the entire planet was hardly better than the farthest-flung of the colonies.

Scavengers regularly visited Earth, scrounging through old urban centers for functional technology and equipment, which would in turn be sold to the poorest of the colonies. Such theft - for there was no better description for the act - made the situation on Earth even worse, depriving the stubborn hold-outs of what remained of their inheritance.

To prevent the looting, Earth's survivors, along with a handful of worlds that had sided with the Homeworld during the Great War, had funded the pitiful Sol Patrol. The militia was a bitter shadow of Earth's grand navy during the war, and it was largely ineffective, but it served its purpose as a deterrent.

Gail was still strapped into the pilot's chair. Meg had never been trained on starship systems, and while Caree had been a captain of her own vessel, she was hardly experienced with practical piloting or gunnery. Rake wasn't happy about someone else piloting his ship, but the skiptracer was competent enough to fly herself around the Expanse. With the recalibrated neural interface now operating smoothly, Rake knew he was ready to fight if someone from the poorly-equipped Sol Patrol stumbled across the gunship.

At least he hoped so. After he had finished the calibration, he had spent a half-hour running through practice routines. On occasion, the interface seemed to blur out. Rake had checked and re-checked the gunnery systems, but every diagnostic had come up green.

Which means it's this body, he told himself. *Something's not right - which I've known since I woke up at Terra. Whatever is wrong, it's only going to keep getting worse, too.* He kept the thought to himself, not wanting to alarm his companions.

After I get clear of this mess, I'm going straight back to the insurance company and demanding they do something about it.

"So what exactly are we looking for here?" Caree asked, her voice tight.

Rake appraised her for a moment.

She's way too tense for something as simple as this. It's not like the Sol Patrol is really a threat to us.

"I'm not sure," he confessed. "It's the last lead we have - I know I was here, but that's it."

"Do you even know whether you were on Earth, or at the moon colony, or the Mars or Venus colonies?" she asked with a bit of frustration. "Maybe you were at one of the refueling stations here? Or at one of the asteroid mines?"

The ex-Terran officer offered a long-suffering sigh. "You're asking questions like Meg," he grumbled. "I really don't know where I was. It's not like I'm going to remember, either - life insurance doesn't work that way."

Meg shot him an angry glare, but he ignored it.

"So, let's do a nice long orbit around the star and see if anything pops," he decided. "I had to have a reason to come here. Maybe I can figure out where I would have stopped. It's not like my mind doesn't still work the same way."

But does it really still work the same way? Your reflexes were off, the neural interface doesn't seem to work right anymore. How do you know your thought processes are still as sharp as they were?

He didn't allow his unease to show as Gail laid in a long orbit around the sun between Earth and Mars, thrusters flaring at full power.

Their initial jump into the system had placed them rather close to Earth, in terms of the vast distances in space. The orbit Gail had plotted would require days at full acceleration to accomplish, but they were hardly a half-hour of travel time from Earth.

The *Mirage* had just begun its run when the radio began beeping incessantly, calling for attention. Gail handled opening the channel, putting it over the cockpit speakers to allow all to listen.

"Weston, is that you?" a voice asked hurriedly. "What are you doing here? I thought we had an agreement!"

Rake exchanged puzzled looks with the three women before answering, "This is Weston," he said cautiously. "Who am I speaking with?"

"You know damned well who you're talking to," the voice on the radio hissed. "Like I said, we had an agreement that you'd stay away! What are you doing here?"

"Searching," Rake said dryly.

The man on the other end seemed confused for a moment. "Searching? For what? What could be so damned important you risked coming back here?"

"After I left here, I died," Rake said shortly, deciding on the direct route. "I'm back from my insurance policy, but I have no idea why the Terrans are chasing me."

The radio was silent for several long moments. "Insurance policy. Great. Were you followed here?"

"No," Rake said confidently. "We slipped our pursuit at Clarion before heading this way. I don't doubt they'll catch up with me again, though - the Terrans have agents everywhere."

"Yes, they do," the other agreed. "So you have no idea why they're all chasing you? And what you knew?"

"No," Rake said. "I've been trying to put together the pieces, but there's too many gaps, and none of the skiptracers or military boys shooting at me have seemed interested in stopping to discuss the matter."

"We had better talk in person, then," the man on the radio decided. "Some things are better not said over the radio, even on encrypted channels. I'm sending you coordinates and clearance codes - please join me as quickly as you can."

Gail offered a thumbs-up to indicate she had received the data. "Talk to you shortly," Rake said, drawing his finger across his throat. The skiptracer closed the channel and leaned back in her chair.

"So, we go talk to this guy?" Meg asked.

"Not 'we'," Rake corrected. "Me. Alone."

"I don't like that idea at all," Gail spoke up. "You're too valuable for me to let you wander around alone."

The pilot shook his head. "It's better this way. I'd bet the ship that I was here alone last time. If something *does* go wrong, you three are my cards up the sleeve - whoever this guy is, he doesn't know about you so he won't be ready for you."

"Wonderful," Caree grumbled. "And what happens if this guy shoots you dead?"

Rake shrugged helplessly. "I don't know why he would. Only people that seem interested in that are Terrans, and it seems pretty far-fetched they'd have someone sitting here just to try to decoy me." He nodded at Gail. "Take us in."

* * *

Their destination was a small station orbiting Earth itself. At first glance, the little platform appeared to be dead and abandoned - there were no external lights, no radio transmissions, and several of the viewports had been cracked or shattered, exposing at least some of the station to hard vacuum.

Closer examination, and a careful analysis of the *Mirage*'s sensor data, showed atmosphere available at a single airlock, and trace power readings from deeper in the station.

Looks like someone keeping his head down, Rake concluded. *Probably my type of guy.*

Docking with the station was a bit trickier than usual. Usually for such operations, guidance systems on the station would interface with the ship's computers to automate most of the process. In this case, however, the station's docking controls were shut down and Gail was forced to bring the ship in manually. Twice Rake was tempted to take the controls from the skiptracer, as the task seemed beyond her ability for precision flying, but he forced himself to refrain.

On Gail's third attempt, the airlocks matched and she locked the ship in place with magnetic grapples. When the ship's engines quieted, the skiptracer turned and offered a shaky smile and thumbs-up to Rake.

Taking it as his cue, the pilot rose from the gunner's chair after disconnecting the neural interface and headed aft to the airlock, stopping only long enough to pick up his sidearm and throw his concealing jacket on again.

Doesn't pay to bother with body armor for this, he told himself. *If this goes bad, I'm probably not going to walk out of there in one piece anyway.*

Meg and Caree were both waiting at the airlock when he arrived. "I still think this is a bad idea," Caree grumbled. "Walking in there by yourself is a good way to get killed or captured. Let me come with you."

"No," Rake said with a firm shake of his head. "If something goes wrong, you and Gail are the ones who can likely get me out of there again. You went toe-to-toe with Slade at Terra, and Gail can fly the ship." He offered an apologetic smile to Meg. "No offense to you."

"None taken," the girl said weakly. "I'd rather not risk my life."

"Me neither," he said with a smile. "So you three keep your heads down and, if things go bad, pull me out of the fire."

Neither of the women offered a quip, just a solemn nod, as Rake tapped the clearance code into the station's airlock controls. With a parting wave, he stepped through into the station and cycled the lock.

The airlock was bone-chilling cold - nearly twenty below, Rake figured.

I should have dressed warmer. I hope the rest of the station isn't freezing like this.

Thankfully, as he hiked down the barely-illuminated corridor, the cold seemed to lose its edge. He could still see his breath when he reached a closed internal door several minutes later, though. It didn't yield to his touch, and the electronic lock was unlit. With no other options available, he knocked.

The boom seemed to reverberate through the entire station, setting his teeth on edge. Nervousness crept up on him, though he knew intellectually it was silly.

This guy's probably the only one here, and it's not like the sound can carry through vacuum. Take it easy, Weston.

You're getting close to figuring this whole thing out. Keep your wits and you'll be fine. If he knows what's going on, this is what you'll need to get clear of this whole mess.

The door silently slid into the wall. "Weston, is that you?" a voice asked.

Rake squinted and tried to see through the gloom into the even-darker chamber beyond. "It's me," he confirmed. "Though I'd like to know who you are."

The room suddenly blazed with brilliant light, and he grimaced as he was blinded by the intense illumination. "Is that necessary?" he asked.

A short, dark-haired man stepped out with a long coilgun aimed at Rake's chest. "Can never be too certain, Weston," he said. "Not with what we're talking about."

"And what exactly is that?" Rake asked.

The man lowered his weapon. "Let's talk," he said, jerking his head back at the brightly lit room before retreating inside.

Rake followed him in; he had barely stepped through when the door hissed shut, cutting off the cold and dark of the long corridor. The warmth was abrupt but welcome, though he was a bit irritated to see condensation beading up on his jacket and sidearm.

Wet clothes and a rusty gun, he thought irritably, *make for an unhappy spacer.*

He glanced around, taking in his surroundings. The chamber was likely the station's old command center, with banks of outdated computer equipment lining the outer walls, and floor-to-ceiling equipment, including dozens of display screens, occupying the very center of the room. A bunk had been mounted to one wall, and nearby was a small food-prep station. *All the comforts of home*, he thought wryly.

"Do you remember who I am?" the short man asked.

Rake shook his head. "I really have no idea at all who you are," he confessed.

"My name is Nik Relis," he said shortly. "You came to me for help decoding some data." He was silent for a moment, clearly pondering his own thoughts, before asking, "So, what *do* you remember?"

"Not much. I updated my memories at my insurance provider at Terra, and *then* I took this job, whatever it was." Rake swallowed. "I woke up a few days ago at the insurance company, and I've been hounded by skiptracers and the Terran military ever since."

"Why did you come to Earth, then?" the little man wanted to know.

"Because it was the only lead I had left." He quickly sketched out what had happened since he awoke, starting with Slade attacking him *inside* the insurance facility, fleeing from the Terrans at Lantash, finding his ship on Clarion, and the few bits of data he'd been able to glean from his computer and from his conversations with Shoram and Wirst. He left out a few details along the way - the imperfections in his new body, dragging Meg off the ring, Caree's survival after the *Starfall*'s destruction, and the presence of the skiptracer Gail on his ship.

"You said there was still data in your navigation system from your jump before Earth?" Nik asked.

Rake shrugged. "It was all scrambled," he said. "They don't point to any known system in the Expanse."

"That's because it *isn't* a known system," Nik said reprovingly. "That's why you came to me for help."

"Not a known system?" the pilot asked dubiously. "There hasn't been any real exploration of new jumps in years."

"No, there hasn't been, but that doesn't mean all the discoveries were public knowledge." Nik's smile was grim. "After the Terran Independence War, the old Earth

Military Force decided they needed a fallback position - secret shipyards, fuel and munition storage, everything they'd need to conduct a war should Earth fall."

Rake frowned thoughtfully. "Why have I never heard of this?" he asked.

"Technically, you had - but then you got yourself killed. But mostly because you were an officer in Terra's navy, not Earth's," Nik supplied. "It was built only a few years before the Great War, and just the ranking officers knew it even existed, let alone where it was. Assignment there was a one-way trip, too - the soldiers stationed there weren't allowed to leave, ever."

"So everyone's looking for this hidden military base," Rake said grimly.

"That wasn't your theory before," Nik contradicted. "You were fairly certain the Lost Fleets were there."

"The Lost Fleets," the pilot repeated, his heart sinking.

"Yep. You had figured that's where both Earth and Terra's fleets disappeared to after Earth was torched. You came here with jump data recorded by a satellite that had survived because it was in the moon's shadow," the little man said. "You needed help calculating for years of galactic expansion and drift." He glared at Rake, open hostility in his eyes. "You also agreed you wouldn't come back here after you'd found it. Of course, you did anyway."

Rake mumbled an apology. "Hard to hold a dead guy to a promise."

"I'm not talking about now," Nik said. "I'm talking about shortly after you'd *been* to the Lost Fleets."

"Wait, I came back immediately after?" he asked.

The little man nodded. "You came back to ask me my advice, because you were worried about Boss Bruno getting his hands on the location," he said tightly. "So you wanted my help sending an open transmission to Boss Bruno that the Terrans would intercept - you figured they'd go after him."

"And they went after me instead," Rake said, his heart already so low he didn't think it could sink any further.

"Exactly."

"So, now what?" Rake asked. "How do we get out of this mess?"

"I already know that," Nik said cheerfully. "One of us had to plan ahead, since the other got killed."

Hope flooded him, and his heart rose at the pronouncement. "So what's our plan?"

Three wall sections slid open, revealing a dozen armed men. "I turn you over to Boss Bruno and walk out of here a wealthy man."

XVII

SLOW CLAPPING FILLED THE CHAMBER. Rake kept his hands up and clear of his jacket, making no move for his partly-concealed sidearm.

Play it cool, he told himself. *You've got your backup sitting nearby on the ship, and these guys don't know anything about them.*

The source of the clapping soon became clear as a heavily-muscled, red-headed man walked around the central bank of computers. "Nicely done, Mr. Relis. You've earned your pay."

"Thank you, Mr. Bruno," Nik said with an inclined head. "I figured you would prefer the whole story voluntarily, instead of interrogating him for it."

"Definitely a time-saver," Boss Bruno agreed. "Mr. Weston, I'm quite disappointed in you. Do you realize you came with such high recommendations from my colleagues? I was rather surprised when you tried to sell me out to the Terrans over the Last Redoubt's location." He shook his head in disgust. "That is bad for business, boy, you know? Such actions would make you unemployable in the outer colonies. You gave up a promising career with your treachery. Pity about that." He offered a small smile. "Fortunately, I now have everything I wanted when I first hired you, though it cost me far more money than it should have."

"You don't have everything," Rake said tightly. "You need my ship for the coordinates, don't you? You don't have that yet."

"Yes, boy, I do," Bruno chided him. "Don't I?"

"Of course," a familiar female voice said from the corridor's portal.

Rake swiveled his head over to look, and his heart fell again. Caree, Meg, and Gail all stood at the entrance. To his shock, however, it was *Caree* who stood with a weapon trained on the other two. "I dumped his ship's navigational logs," she added, tossing a small data wafer casually toward Bruno. "If Nik does his magic here, we'll have the coordinates to the Last Redoubt in a few minutes. Correcting for a week or two of drift is far different than correcting for years."

Nik picked the wafer off the floor and silently took it to a computer to begin the drift calculations.

Rake glowered at Boss Bruno as he began to put the pieces together. "I never sent for Caree here, did I? She was working for you from the beginning."

"Of course. I wouldn't risk sending a skiptracer into an insurance facility like the Terrans," he added with a snort. "Clumsy and foolish of them. Just because they're the biggest fish left in the pond, they think they can stomp on everyone else. I also wasn't happy about my assets they destroyed at the Lantash Six ring, either."

The pilot shook his head. "That's why I never heard anything from any of your people, even with the bounty posted for me," he reflected. "You were allowing for an independent to pick me up if push came to shove, but you didn't need to send any of your people because you already had one there." He sighed, despair starting to sink in. "And she's been keeping you aware of our movements, which is how you beat me here."

"I had already uncovered Nik here as the source for your little broadcast to the Terrans," Bruno corrected. "He's rather mercenary, you know - you shouldn't have trusted him without payment up front. Then it was just a matter of waiting for you to show up here."

"So now what?" Rake asked tightly. "You have the coordinates, so you execute me?"

"Hardly," Bruno said with a laugh. "If I did that, you'd wind up in the hands of the Terrans, and until I've secured the Last Redoubt I can hardly have that, even without your memories." He shook his head firmly, the decision clearly already made. "It took you a handful of days to find your way back here - with the Terrans prompting you, I bet you could find your way even faster."

"How could I wind up in the Terrans' hands?" Rake asked in disbelief. "It's not like I could afford another insurance policy."

"Not that you could afford the first one, either," Bruno corrected him. "I knew all about your little sordid past with the Terran navy, and saw that there was potential in you - and losing you would have been such a waste. How do you think you got the policy in the first place?" Bruno waved his hand dismissively. "After your little escapade at Lantash, the Terrans paid to renew your policy and then switched to a kill order on you. They believed it could keep you out of my hands and ensure you were back in their own."

Rake shook his head in disbelief, but it all tracked clean.

Well, that's one positive about this whole thing. I've still got a policy out there if I get killed.

He swallowed hard as he kept tracking through the logic.

Of course, they can only activate my policy if I'm confirmed dead. If he takes me out to the Lost Fleets and kills me there with no one around, there's no body - and no report to get the new body released. I'll be dead for good.

"So, what are you going to do with me?" Rake asked casually.

"I can't risk the Terrans catching up with you," Bruno said cheerfully. "I also can't risk someone seeing us space you or drop you in a star, so I keep you alive and with me for now. Once I have the Last Redoubt, we'll determine an adequate punishment for you."

Rake glanced at Gail and Meg before asking, "And them?"

"I don't want to kill you and risk the Terrans waking you up, so they're leverage," the crime lord said brusquely. "Cooperate and they'll be fine; be disagreeable, and we'll have issues." He glanced over at Gail, studying her with interest. "Unless, of course, you'd prefer to be on my payroll," he offered. "You were good enough to catch Weston not once, but twice. I could use someone of your talent working for me."

The skiptracer offered a tight smile. "Well, this is worth discussing," she said. "After all, if it weren't for me, the Terrans would have killed him on Clarion. You pay me the reward for his capture and delivery, and we can discuss further employment opportunities."

Rake's temper flared and he snarled, "You back-blading bitch! You told me..."

"Money speaks louder than words," she interrupted smoothly, dismissing him entirely as she watched Bruno. "Do we have a deal?"

"Done and done," he said with a small smile. "You see, Weston? This is how business people work. It can't be personal - it's about profit."

"Yeah," Rake grumbled, "profit."

"Drift corrections are complete," Nik announced, offering up a handful of data wafers. "Here's all the navigational data you will need to jump to and from the Last Redoubt."

"Thank you," Bruno said gracefully as he took the wafers. "The money will be deposited in your accounts upon my return." He offered a frosty smile. "You understand I must confirm the delivery before I pay out."

"Perfectly," Nik said with a nod.

"Excellent. Now, I can hardly afford to leave Weston's ship here," he said, stroking his chin. "Gail, I believe Caree mentioned you were capable of piloting it, correct? I would like you and two of my men to accompany Weston. Caree, you and that girl will come with me on my vessel." He offered a small smile. "Understand that, should any harm come to Rake, it will reflect poorly on any future employment opportunities between us."

The blue-haired woman nodded once. "Of course, Mr. Bruno."

"Good. Now, let us be off."

* * *

The walk down the passageway was cold and silent. For the first time since he woke up in the insurance facility, he felt completely helpless.

My "friends" have all turned on me, except Meg, and she's worthless in this except as blackmail. I'm held at gunpoint on my own ship, and Bruno got what he was looking for. In a few minutes we'll confirm the location of the Lost Fleets, and then I'll probably be executed. With no confirmation of my death, the insurance company will never bring me back.

This is the end of Rake Weston. He swallowed hard as he walked through the airlock, perhaps for the last time, into his ship. *I lost, and badly. I trusted the wrong people, and now a crime lord is going to get his hands on the deadliest weapon in the Expanse.* He tried telling himself it wasn't his fault, but he couldn't make himself believe it. *Once you had the information, you should've destroyed it - blew up your ship, killed Nik, killed yourself. That would have been better than letting Bruno get his hands on it.*

I failed.

"I want him in the cockpit," Gail announced coolly. "Tie him into the gunner's chair. Restrain his hands, so he can't reach any controls, and we'll be fine."

"Why?" the larger of Bruno's thugs asked.

"In case something goes wrong," the skiptracer said. "The weapons on this thing are all setup with a neural link, and he's the only one who can use it. If we get jumped by Terrans, I want to shoot back."

Both of the bruisers grumbled under their breaths, but followed the skiptracer's orders. A few minutes later, Rake was bound to the chair, the bands so tight he could hardly move beyond his breathing.

Gail seated herself in the pilot's chair, quickly running through the ship's preflight. The *Mirage* steadily came to life under her fingertips, the engines sending a familiar vibration throughout the ship. She nodded to herself as she worked, humming some old music under her breath.

Rake could do nothing but watch and listen. He glanced over at the neural interface cable, coiled up neatly on the console next to him.

If only I could reach over and plug it in, or talk Gail into connecting me. If nothing else, I could get a shot at Bruno's ship. My coilguns are powerful enough to probably take him in the first shot.

But nothing he could think of would work. He was short on money after exercising his credit line on several worlds, so bribery was right out. Threats were unlikely to work, given his current bound state. Sex appeal wasn't something that would work with Bruno's very male thugs, and Gail was too professional. He had yet to think of a scenario where he could *trick* them into it, and he somehow doubted asking nicely would end well.

Yep, you're screwed.

And then, just to make things worse, the proximity alarm began to blare.

Gail was frantically tapping buttons on the console. "Terran ships just jumped in!" she shouted. "They're practically on top of us! How'd they get that close?"

Rake grimaced. "Standard military tactic for the Terrans," he said. "Jump to a point about twenty light-minutes out from your target. Run the numbers, adjust for the time it takes the light to reach you, and jump right onto your target before light can return to it."

Gail swung her chair around to look at the two thugs. "Plug him in," she snarled. "We need to be able to shoot back!"

Rake grimaced as one of the bruisers roughly jammed the neural interface cable into the jack, but managed to keep himself quiet. Gail was initializing the link, but it would take several seconds - lifetimes, really - before he would be able to interpret the data and aim the weapons.

"I can't release the airlock from here," Gail said sharply. "I need one of you back there right now so we can get free."

The smaller of the two nodded silently and immediately headed aft.

Rake fought down the flood of adrenaline in his system as he tried to interpret the gunship's data link.

Come on, come on, calm down or it'll interfere with the system, he told himself. *Just wait for the data before you panic.*

The intercom beeped. "I'm back here at the airlock, but I don't see the release," the thug began. "Do you know where it is?"

"Just a second," Gail said.

The jumble of data from the ship's sensors began to unfold in Rake's mind. He could still see with his eyes, of course, but he was very much seeing *past* the ship bulkheads, out into space, where pinpoints of colored light represented satellites, ships, debris. *Wait, what?* was the only thought he managed.

Then Gail jammed the throttle forward.

The *Mirage* screamed, a horrible sound of ripping metal as the mated airlocks were torn asunder. A horrible screeching wind followed on its heels, and loose objects around the cockpit were picked up and vanished in the stream of air.

Gail turned smoothly in her chair, and Rake barely caught a glimpse of her before her terrible sidearm, the weapon she called a Dagon, discharged with a loud *crack*.

Rake was bound too tightly to do anything but take the blow. Except it never came, and a meaty thump was audible even over the roar of escaping air. He managed to swivel the gunner's chair just enough to see the feet of the now-prone bruiser.

The rush of wind vanished as emergency bulkheads slammed shut, sending echoing booms throughout the *Mirage*, audible even in the rapidly thinning atmosphere.

Rake shook his head as the gunship rocketed away from the station. He focused on the sensor data again, but it revealed the same thing it had before: absolutely nothing.

Gail hunched over the pilot's console in spite of the acceleration pushing both of them back in their seats. "We had an agreement," she said as way of explanation. "Neither of us want Bruno to get his hands on the Catalyst."

"Then we need to go back and blow him out of space," Rake said roughly. "This ship can take anything he can field."

"He's already gone," Gail said. "He jumped right before I tore us away from the station. Looks like he wasn't going to waste any time."

Rake gritted his teeth. "Then it's too late."

"Maybe, maybe not," Gail said. "Yes, he has the Lost Fleets, but there's probably hundreds of ships to search. Even if he calls in a big part of his organization, it'll take time to search for it." The skiptracer shrugged, more than a bit helpless. "We've got a little time left, but I don't know how to use it."

Rake's pulse slowed as he began to consider their options in light of the unexpected reversal. "Well, I'm pretty sure I can't call up enough friends to go up against Bruno and whatever of his thugs he took with him. Can you?"

The skiptracer shook her head. "No. Not since the Guild dissolved, and even then I'd have to come up with something to pay them. It'd take me a month or more to put together a group of fighters ready to do this."

Rake blew out a deep breath. "Guess we've really only got one option, then." He offered a small smile. "It's so stupid it just might work."

XVIII

"THIS IS THE CRAZIEST THING I've ever done," Gail commented wryly from the pilot's chair. "Seriously, this is absolutely *mad*. This is crazier than that hunt I took on Piera II."

"I heard about that, I think," Rake commented from the gunner's chair. "That fire, in the dome on Piera II's fourth moon, right?"

"That was the end of it, yeah," the skiptracer said. "I haven't been back since. Pretty sure they'd still shoot me on sight."

"Or pin a medal on you." Rake shook his head. "How long?"

"Point drive is spun up and ready to go," she reported, her tone instantly professional. "We're less than two minutes away from our planned entry window." Her voice became more casual as she added, "You know, I've heard

216

good things about you - that you're a professional, that you're a soldier, and that when you have time to plan, you can manage damn near anything. This is still utterly crazy, though."

"Do we have another choice?" Rake asked as he ran through a final check of the *Mirage*'s weapons systems, confirmed his neural link. He nodded to himself when everything came up with full readiness.

"No, we're short on options," she agreed. "Doesn't make this any less crazy."

The two fell into a companionable silence as they waited. Rake added a small timer to the neural link, and suddenly had a small clock floating in the corner of his vision, counting down the seconds. As it neared zero, he unlocked all the weapons systems, his hands gripped on the additions to his gunner's chair - a pair of control sticks to aid precise aiming and firing.

Then the *Mirage* jumped.

Rake grimaced at the ripping sensation, clinging hard to consciousness. It threatened to slip away in spite of his efforts, but he fought like a madman to stay awake. An eternity later, his mind cleared and he was still aware.

The *Mirage* was already tumbling through space as Gail began maneuvering. He tried to ignore the nausea-inducing sway and instead concentrated on the neural link.

The ship's sensors fed him data, information his brain translated into images. He closed his eyes to lose the visual distraction of the ship's cockpit and instead watched space around them, painted on the inside of his eyelids.

Hundreds of contacts lit up the ship's sensors all around them. He could see them, in a way - visual images provided by either the ship's computer, his memory, or both. Ships were illuminated with various colors - red for known hostiles, blue for presumed friendlies, green for neutralized vessels. Weapons fire, almost invisible in the darkness of space, was illuminated as brilliant yellow flashes, revealing active conflicts across the system.

When Boss Bruno had vanished with the location of the Lost Fleets, Rake had known there was likely only one way to stop him, and had made a single longcast to Colonel Velles.

The Terran Navy was a shadow of its former self, but it was still more than enough to take on a crime lord who had grown too big for his boots.

"We've got a pair of Terran fighters coming our way," Gail called tightly. "They probably saw the radiation surge when we jumped in. ECM and ECCM are both spinning up, and the bandits are trying to jam us. Looks like it'll be visual targeting only."

"Great, activate Seasick and let it do the flying," Rake ordered. "And paint me some targets."

White concentric rings appeared in Rake's vision, highlighting the intercepting fighters. He smiled tightly as he slid a small crosshair across the first craft and tightened his fingers on the control sticks' triggers.

The *Mirage*'s weapons systems were experimental, designed to allow a single officer to handle the entire array. Due to the size and shape of the vessel, however, there was no way for all of the weapons to fire at an individual target. Simply put, at any given time some of the coilguns could not fire at a target without hitting the *Mirage* itself. The fire control computer handled the heavy lifting, engaging safeties to prevent the vessel from shooting itself, allowing the gunner to focus wholly on tracking and attacking targets.

Four of the *Mirage's* six coilguns opened fire at Rake's bidding. The tiny projectiles were virtually invisible, but the neural interface painted an estimated picture of their trajectory and location, right up until the lead fighter shattered.

Rake swung his crosshair over the second interceptor, but the pilot was already evading. Seasick was evading, too - Rake could feel the ship's violent maneuvers, though his vision remained steady as he offered a few bursts from the guns to keep his remaining opponent at bay.

"Rake?" Gail's voice was in his ear. "I've got a match on the old Terran flagship. It looks like there's a firefight going on over there between some Terran warships and the old ship itself."

Rake grunted as he tried again to tag the starfighter, which was managing to close the gap in spite of its violent evasive maneuvers. "So Bruno managed to get at least one of the ships running, huh?" he commented between clenched teeth.

"More than one," the skiptracer reported. "Apparently the two days it took the Terrans to get their fleet here was way too long."

"But we were sitting in orbit around Saturn almost the entire time," Rake commented skeptically. "If he would have brought a bunch of ships with technicians and crew in, we would have noticed, wouldn't we?"

"Maybe he had a cargo hold full of AIs," Gail commented. "I mean, if they got a couple of the cruisers up and running, you wouldn't need to have much more than point and shoot - the Terrans don't have anything big enough to take on a couple cruisers."

"Wonderful," Rake grumbled. The fighter had closed to a range he could finally pick out the details - a sleek, flying-wing craft he was unfamiliar with. Seasick seemed to detect an opening, and abruptly the *Mirage* went into a hard forward acceleration. The starfighter pilot accelerated in response, his movements smooth and precise. He didn't have time to realize his mistake before Rake was firing again, and the *Mirage*'s guns ripped him apart. "Stick with the plan."

"Great. The plan. You're sure this is going to work?"

"If you want *sure*, settle on Terra and pay your taxes. You agreed with me that Bruno getting his hands on the Catalyst was a bad thing, right? If we don't act, either he or the Terrans will get it, and I don't doubt either one will use it." Rake scanned the skies for more contacts, but no one else seemed to be paying them attention - at least not yet.

"Doesn't mean I can't have second thoughts," Gail muttered.

"Worry later, act now," he ordered. "Once we're on the flagship, we're not going to have a lot of time to get Meg out and steal the Catalyst. If we can slip in while they're not paying us any attention, our chances are far better."

"If we survive this, I'm going to spend a month at some beach resort where clothing is prohibited," Gail said tightly. "And you're paying for it."

"If we survive this," Rake replied, "I'll join you."

"Sure, you won't sleep with me *before* certain death, but *afterward*," the blue-haired woman riposted.

"Who said anything about sleeping with you?"

The old Terran flagship, resurrected by Bruno's crew, was a monstrosity - nearly a kilometer long and armed with dozens of weapons, including coilguns large enough to destroy the *Mirage* with a single shot. It was operational but clearly crippled, an entire third of the warship's hull open to space and lacking atmosphere.

And still the Terran warships were keeping their distance. Three destroyers circled the supercruiser, their weapons pounding away to little effect. The flagship fired in return, but ineffectually - whether it was because of poor AI, miscalibrated equipment, or simple battle damage, Rake could not tell. Still, the destroyers were in no hurry to close the gap and expose themselves to more accurate fire from the supercruiser's heavy guns.

The *Mirage*, under Seasick's guidance, closed the gap quickly. Whoever was monitoring the old flagship's sensors apparently either missed or ignored them; no coilguns threatened their approach, no alerts flared from the sensors from a targeting lock. *This is almost too easy*, Rake thought.

The nearest Terran destroyer opened up on them instead.

The *Mirage* shuddered as small anti-starfighter flak hammered the hull. The fire was too light, the hull too heavily armored, and the gunship moving too slow for it to be a crippling blow, but it sent the little vessel off-course. The AI tried to compensate, but the engine misfirings kept it from straightening their flight path.

They were too close to their destination, to near the end, for Rake to sit and watch from the gunner's chair. Instead of waiting for the neural interface to gracefully shut down, he reached back and ripped the cable from his jack. Pain flared through his brain and would have sent him to his knees, had he been standing.

He blinked several times as he fumbled with the chair's straps, trying to adjust from his perception of space and starships to the cramped cockpit instead. The abrupt disconnect left him dizzy and he nearly fell when he managed to shrug out of his harness; the next engine misfire *did* send him tumbling to the cold, hard deck.

Gail turned at the noise of his crash, cursed, and unstrapped herself from the pilot's chair. She reached down to help him, but he was already lunging up and barely made it into the seat before the ship jerked again, this time sending Gail to her hands and knees.

Rake didn't bother strapping in before disengaging the AI's control and dropping his hands on the yoke. His eyes were scanning the diagnostic displays as he began to fight the controls.

The port engine was misfiring frequently, while the starboard drive showed no problems. The center engine, too, was unsteady, though it provided more power than the crippled port drive.

"Hang on," he said belatedly, "because this is going to get ugly." He released the throttle for just a moment to cut fuel to both starboard and port drives, leaving only the centerline engine to provide thrust.

The vessel steadied its swaying, but the random bursts from the remaining drive slammed Rake repeatedly into the pilot's chair. "Remind me to reprogram that damned pilot AI," Rake growled, "so that it's smart enough to cut power to malfunctioning engines."

"If I don't break my neck in here, I will," Gail offered up painfully as she finally crawled into the gunner's chair. "That hurt."

"I imagine it did," Rake grunted. "Have you transmitted the codes yet?"

"No, I just had the shortcast queued up when we took that hit."

Rake's hands were tightly clamped around the yoke and throttle. "Do it from there," he decided as the *Mirage* bucked yet again. "I don't want to let go here."

"Don't you think the Terrans already tried this?" Gail asked dubiously. "I mean, it seems like an obvious thing to do. Radio the emergency clearance codes and land in the hangar?"

"They would have, if they could," Rake answered. "Terran security protocol denies any ships outside a task force access to the clearance codes - which means they wouldn't have been stored on Terra, either. Unless they've got one of the other ships that survived, they don't have the codes."

"I'm getting an automated reply," Gail said tightly. "I'll be damned. Door for the ventral landing bay is opening."

"Great," he muttered. "Now we just need to get there."

The approach to the emergency bay was a pilot's nightmare. The supercruiser's own guns were not an issue - this close in, the *Mirage*'s computer could warn Rake if any coilguns took a bead on them. The real danger laid in the three attacking destroyers and their weapons, all aimed at the old flagship. The high-velocity rounds falling on the warship were too fast and too frequent to be adequately detected on sensors. It would be all too possible for the *Mirage* to blindly wander into one of their fire lanes and be torn to shreds by the heavy cannons before the gunship's crew was aware of the danger.

White-knuckled, Rake took the *Mirage* in.

Closing the gap took just under twenty seconds. It wasn't the longest twenty seconds Rake had ever experienced - he had been a combat pilot with the Terran navy during the Great War, and he was intimately aware of how slowly time could pass while in combat.

He didn't remember ever feeling more helpless.

Rake was hyper-aware during the approach; every creak, every strained rivet, was a sign of imminent doom; every misfire from the lone operating engine, every vibration in the controls, every stray groan in the decking was a harbinger of death.

Then the twenty seconds was past, and the *Mirage* was inside the supercruiser's hangar.

The doors began to grind shut even before the gunship's tail was through, sealing once more against the vacuum of space and the combat surrounding the ship.

The bay was large and dimly-lit, but Rake could make out some detail anyway. A sleek shuttle, most likely Bruno's personal craft, was parked against a wall, with a much larger armed freighter parked next to it like a protective parent. Besides those craft, however, the hangar was chaos.

Old Terran fighters and bombers were strewn across the decks. Most of them had been thrown from their hardstands; only a handful remained upright and looked flyable. Several old military shuttles had also been tipped over and laid on their sides, the deck beneath them long-ago stained with dark fluids no doubt leaked from failing seals and split hoses.

Rake gave up on finding a clear space large enough to accommodate the *Mirage*. Extending the landing gear, he set the gunship down, wincing at the crunches and vibrations running through the vessel as it settled into place.

"I'll be damned," Gail breathed. "We actually made it. I didn't think we'd survive the run in - between Bruno's people and the Terran navy, I was sure someone would kill us."

"Just remember," Rake said with a small smile as he rotated the pilot's chair around and rose to his feet, "that was the easy part. It's going to get uglier from here."

The skiptracer grimaced. "Weren't you an officer? Don't they give you lessons in motivating your troops, or anything like that?"

"Here's some motivation," Rake offered. "If we pull this off, we both get to live."

"Works for me. Let's go steal a weapon and rescue a damsel in distress."

XIX

THERE WERE A HANDFUL OF Bruno's thugs on the hangar deck, all dead or unconscious from decompression. Gail checked them individually, prodding them with the barrel of her Dagon and applying liberal blunt force to the skulls of any that seemed near consciousness.

Rake didn't bother protesting – her method seemed less cruel than the alternative: shoot any that still had a pulse.

"Are you done?" he asked impatiently.

"Nearly," she assured him. "Last thing we want is for any of these boys to wake up and interrupt the job."

"That's why we're wearing armor," Rake said dryly, poking himself in the chest.

"This is just the light stuff. Doesn't make us invincible. I wish you would have had a couple of suits of power armor, though," Gail griped. "I'd feel a lot better about this plan of yours if we had the heavy stuff."

"So would I, but all I've got on the ship is a loader suit for handling munitions. My usual jobs mean I try to avoid suspicion, and it's hard to look innocent when you're armed and armored head to toe."

"Why bother looking innocent if no one has the firepower to stop you?"

"I think we'll have to agree to disagree," Rake said dryly.

"So, now what?" Gail asked as she straightened from applying a solid whack with the butt of her Dagon to the last of Bruno's help.

"We stick with the plan. Find the weapon, find Meg, and get the hell out of this warzone." Rake resettled his jacket, only partly concealing the added bulk of the body armor, and unholstered his sidearm. "As bad as the plan may be, we stick to it."

"I *did* mention I dislike this plan, right?"

"Only a dozen times or so."

The launch tubes and hangars were the lowest decks on the ship. The supercruiser was actually an old design, with all decks having the same gravity orientation; later warships were designed around a central gravitation axis, with decks both "above" and "below" oriented with their feet toward that axis.

The lift tubes were an extension of the same artificial gravity technology prevalent on all starships. Under normal conditions, microgravity would pull a user toward one end or the other - up or down, relatively speaking. The tubes themselves, if they lost power, would lack gravity completely, making them perfectly safe to traverse.

Comfortable in his understanding of the technology, Rake felt safe as the tube lifted both Gail and him toward their destination: the command center.

Located in the heart of the warship, the command center - called the battle bridge by war journalists, and by extension the common public - was the best-defended, best-equipped part of the ship. It was not uncommon for the command center to survive the destruction of a ship, complete with a living bridge crew. Even with the damage the supercruiser had suffered in its last battle, Rake had no doubt the command center was still serviceable.

He wasn't disappointed.

The two thugs guarding the entrance to the command center were unprepared for Rake and Gail's arrival. Two shots later, and the corridor was empty.

Rake *was* surprised to find the portal to the command center was locked open. In combat conditions, the entrance was always sealed as a safeguard against fire or sudden decompression. Now, against all military protocols, it stood open.

The ex-officer didn't hesitate to walk onto the battle bridge, sidearm in hand and jacket flaring out behind him, confident in his skills, his weapon, his body armor, and his plan. Oh, and the skiptracer in his wake with a Dagon didn't hurt, either.

The nearest of Bruno's men never had a chance. Neither Rake nor Gail held back, raking the bridge with small-arms fire. Six of them went down immediately; the rest either dove for cover or fled toward the far end of the command center.

Gail fired her Dagon, and a thug who had been peeking past a console went down in a bloody mess. "Hurry up, will you?"

"Bruno!" Rake shouted across the confused noise of a ship in combat. "Bruno, you bastard, where is she?" He let the challenge hang in the air as he dropped into a chair and immediately began pulling up data on the nearest screen. "Where is it, where is it?"

"Where is whom, Mr. Weston?" the cultured tones of the crime lord asked, unseen but clearly nearby. "And why are you here? Haven't you already done enough damage?"

"I came here for the girl," he snarled in reply. His voice dropped to a near whisper when he added, "I've got it. Looks like the Catalyst is locked up in armory number four, and nothing's disturbed it yet."

"Transmitting the location now," Gail murmured in return.

"You *were* the one who summoned the Terrans, weren't you, Weston?" Bruno observed casually. "That's the only reason I was going to hold you - until I'd had time to secure the prize. I already let the girl go, back on Earth; she didn't know enough to be dangerous to my plans, and holding her would only have complicated matters."

Rake blinked several times as he looked up from the terminal. "Wait, *what?*"

"I already had the information I needed. I didn't need leverage over you; thanks to you and your ship, I had the coordinates. All I wanted was to keep you out of the way to ensure the Terrans didn't interfere. How you talked the skiptracer into helping you, with your paltry credit accounts, I have no idea."

Gail's voice was heavy with sarcasm. "Well, I felt guilty working for such a law-abiding and respectable citizen, my own reputation what it is. I couldn't risk ruining my good name, so backblading you seemed like such a better idea."

"I'll keep that in mind the next time I offer an open bounty," the criminal said disdainfully. "You know, there used to be honor among people like us - word was as good as law."

"Don't delude yourself," Rake said bluntly. "There's *never* been honor among our kind - only self-interest. Sometimes that self-interest may have meant protecting someone else, or living up to your word, but it's still just *self-interest*, Oscar."

"Pity." The crime boss stepped into view from behind a smoking console, training a lethal-looking longcoil on the pair at the console. "And now here you are, working for the Terrans."

"The Terrans?" Gail laughed, even as the she trained her own weapon on Bruno. "Yeah, something like that. We're both really Terran agents."

"Why are you here, then?" the man demanded.

"I told you, we came for the girl," Rake said as he rose to his feet, moving slowly. He picked up his sidearm from the console and fired three times, the projectiles smashing through circuit boards and screens. *No sense letting him know we've found it.*

The crime lord glanced from the skiptracer to the pilot and back. "Fine. Your prize isn't here. Leave."

"You're just going to let us walk away?" Gail asked skeptically.

"A confrontation will end with death," Bruno said gruffly. "There is no profit for me to kill you here, and a small chance you would win. So, get out and don't come back. I would appreciate if you didn't kill any more of my men. Out, before I change my mind."

Rake and Gail exchanged glances before slowly backing out of the battle bridge, the skiptracer covering them both. "Next time, Bruno," Rake called as the duo backed into the lift tube.

"Next time, Weston," the crime lord said tightly.

As the pair descended, the skiptracer finally commented. "Well, *that* didn't go as planned."

The pilot shook his head wearily. "When does anything?" he asked philosophically. "At least Meg is safe and clear of this mess."

"That sounds like a very good plan for ourselves," Gail said. "I'd really, really like to get us out of here, too."

"That beach without clothes is sounding like a great plan," Rake agreed.

"I haven't decided whether you're invited," the skiptracer countered. "After all, you already scorned me once."

"I wouldn't consider it scorning. More...bad timing. I wasn't expecting it."

"Tsk, tsk, Weston," she said, waggling her finger at him. "Didn't anyone ever tell you to take advantage when you have the chance? You would have made a *terrible* skiptracer."

"Guess that's why I'm just a pilot."

"So, why didn't you kill him?" Gail asked.

"And here I thought you'd appreciate walking out of there alive," he said dryly.

"Oh, I do, don't get me wrong," she said, "but everything about your policy not working because there's no body...well, it'd be the same for him, too. You think the Terran military is going to haul his body back so they can bring his new body off ice? I don't think so."

Rake shrugged uncomfortably as they neared the hangar deck. "It seemed pointless," he said reluctantly. "I mean, yeah, we could've blown his head off, and maybe even gotten out of there alive. But it wouldn't have changed anything - whether he's alive or dead has nothing to do with us getting away with the Catalyst. In fact, dead might have made it more complicated."

Even as he said the words, something seemed wrong - as though he'd made a mistake somewhere, a wrong assumption or perhaps let loose some critical bit of information. He couldn't imagine what it was, though.

His hands and feet were both tingling, which distracted him further.

How much longer is this body going to hold out? he wondered. *All this tingling…is my nervous system completely failing? It was my reflexes that didn't work right.*

Rake and Gail stepped out of the lift tube together, the former still trying to pinpoint what mistake he'd made - if any. He was so caught up in it that he was unprepared when Gail hit him a flying tackle, sending them both sprawling across the hangar deck behind a stack of lubricant drums.

"What?" was all Rake managed before a steady *ping-ping-ping* alerted him to the danger. He grimaced as wetness trickled down on him, lubricant leaking out of the now-bullet-riddled barrels offering him shelter.

"Just one man," Gail said tightly. "In power armor, looks like. See, if we could have suited up for this…"

"Shut up and let me think," he growled, pawing for the small radio he usually kept in his pocket. It was still there, but smashed by the life-saving dive to the floor.

So much for that idea.

"We've got to move," she was saying. "Either he'll keep shooting through the barrels until we're dead, or he'll flank us. We can't stay here. C'mon, Rake, *move.*"

The steady *rattle* of coilgun rounds suddenly fell away. A moment later, a filtered mechanical voice asked, "Rake? Rake *Weston?*"

"Yes," Rake replied brilliantly.

"So, you sold out to Bruno in the end," the voice said disgustedly. "If I would have known you were going to do that, I'd have shot you myself before you escaped Terra. Such a shame - I can kill you now but it won't make a bit of difference anymore."

"Great, then don't kill me," Rake said helpfully, his brain finally catching up with the implications, his heart starting to drop.

This won't end well.

"I don't have a choice," the other said calmly. "I was hired to help secure this vessel, and you're standing in my way."

"No, I'm not," the pilot said, trying to remain calm. He glanced over at Gail, saw she had her Dagon in-hand and ready to fire. Rake shook his head once to slow her.

If we jump out and try to take him, he'll mow us down. "I'm not working for Bruno, and I'm just leaving."

"If you're not working for him, why did you give him the location of the Last Redoubt?"

"If I was working for him, why would I have given your Terran bosses the location, too?" Rake countered. "Bruno got the coordinates out of my ship's computer, not from me. I'm not working for him, and all I want to do is leave." *It's close enough to the truth, anyway*, he told himself.

The mechanical voice laughed, an utterly humorless, cold sound that was doubly harsh with the filtered tones. "Goodbye, Weston."

Rake lunged forward into the drums, heaving with all his strength. Gail joined him an instant later, understanding lighting her face. Even as the *ping-ping-ping* resumed, the drums began to wobble.

And then they fell.

The cavernous hangar echoed with booms as the barrels crashed down, rolling to and fro. Rake stayed low and kept pushing as more and more of the barrels tipped from the stack, until the entire pile had toppled to the deck.

Slade, in full power armor, was flat on his back, struggling to regain his feet after the unexpected crash of drums. The downed man saw the pilot and raised his armed and armored gauntlet to aim. Rake had no time to think, only react, as he threw himself forward at the skiptracer.

It was an insane action - grappling with a man in power armor was as useless a gesture as attacking a starship with his sidearm, and far more likely to get himself killed. No matter how strong or clever he was, Rake would be unable to harm the armored skiptracer in hand-to-hand combat.

Still on his back, however, the skiptracer couldn't bring any weapons to bear in melee combat. Instead, he wrapped his metal-sheeted arms around Rake and began to squeeze. The servo-driven armor began to crush the life out of the unprotected pilot with no more effort than stepping on a bug.

Rake nearly fumbled as the arms closed around him like vices, but in spite of the tingling in his hands, he maintained his grip on his sidearm and swung it up inside Slade's grip. Resting the barrel of the weapon against the skiptracer's armored chin, he smiled faintly and said, "Boom."

The thunderclap of the weapon drove them both apart, Rake's ears ringing from the close-quarters impact of projectile-on-armor as he rolled across the hangar deck. The skiptracer went completely limp.

"That was the most amazingly *stupid* thing I've seen in years," Gail declared cheerfully as she helped Rake back to his feet. "I've been hunting since before the Great War ended, and I've *never* seen someone *charge* a man in full power armor."

"Don't worry," he rasped, "I'm not going to make a habit of it." He reached up and dabbed blood from his face, no doubt drawn by fragments of his bullet. "I was counting on Slade not having seen that, either."

"This is *Slade*?" Gail asked incredulously.

"Yeah, he's kind of been chasing me around since I woke up." Rake grimaced as he looked down at the fallen skiptracer. "Is he dead?"

Gail knelt and worked a finger inside a seam of his armor to feel for a pulse. "No, but he's going to wake up with a hell of a headache."

"Let's get going, then," the pilot grunted. "The sooner we can be off this ship and away from both the Terrans and Bruno, the better."

Gail frowned. "Don't you want to eliminate him first?"

"He was just doing a job," he replied with a miniscule shrug. "I'm not much for executing people."

"He might come after you, just on principle - if you've really slipped him twice."

"If he does, I'll deal with it *then*. For now, he can live."

A shadow fell across them, the outline of another armored figure. Rake and Gail both turned on him with weapons in hand.

"Are you kids coming?" Shoram asked impatiently. "First you make me load up this damned bomb by myself, and now you're standing around discussing morality when there's a damned shooting war going on outside!"

"Yeah, yeah, we're coming," Rake grumbled. "No problem getting it?"

"Not in this loader suit," the old man said with a twinkle in his eye. "Ripped the armory door clear off and carried that weapon back before Slade here blew open an outer hangar door. The failsafes closed it off, but he had plenty of time to get inside first."

Rake looked from the old man to the blue-haired skiptracer. "Let's finish this."

* * *

The primary at the heart of the Last Redoubt's system was scarily close, a relatively young cosmic body - a protostar within a few thousand years of collapsing into its main sequence. In most inhabited systems, the radiation and heat from a star that close would kill anyone in as tight an orbit as the Lost Fleet, but the very young star had yet to begin outputting the amount of energy that would make it lethal.

In the two days Rake and Gail had planned, they had ultimately agreed on two important points: first, they needed help; second, the Catalyst was too dangerous to keep. For the former point, Rake had asked the recently-revived Shoram to join them on their mission. Fresh from his own insurance policy, he had first reviewed *how* he had died, and then only agreed on helping the duo after Rake had explained what they were after.

"If you get me killed a second time, Weston, don't bother coming to me for help again," the old man had warned him. "I don't care how good the cause is; even I can only afford so much insurance."

On the latter point, Rake and Gail had agreed that the weapon had to be destroyed. They also needed to ensure neither Bruno nor the Terrans had reason to believe the weapon still existed, which meant a very public demonstration.

Seasick handled the piloting duties as Shoram, Gail, and Rake prepared the warhead.

The warhead looked so...plain. Rake wasn't sure what he had expected, but a simple titanium-armored missile certainly didn't fit the bill. A serial number was painted on the side, along with a single word: CATALYST.

It was a weapon that could end entire civilizations.

It was terrifying.

Shoram, still strapped into the loader suit, waited as Rake and Gail fueled and armed the weapon. When they had finished, he picked up the missile and loaded it into one of the *Mirage*'s three missile launchers.

When they had finished, Gail returned to the pilot's seat. Rake took up the gunnery chair one last time. The neural interface was uncomfortable this time, and traces of white static seemed to eat at his vision as he looked out through the ship's sensors.

"We're in range," Gail reported grimly. "No one's paying any attention to us."

"Time to change that. Do you have our jump back to Earth plotted?"

"Already done," the skiptracer confirmed. "Drive will be finished spinning up by the time we fire."

"Good." Rake closed his eyes, though it did nothing to cut off the data flowing over the neural link. "Then let's do this." Opening his eyes again, he set the radio for an unencrypted widecast that would reach every ship in the system.

"This is Rake Weston," he announced himself, forcing his voice to remain steady. "I have the remaining Catalyst weapon aboard my ship, taken from the old Terran flagship. This is what you all have been looking for.

"I've armed the weapon and I'm preparing to fire it into the protostar. When it activates, the gravitic profile of the system will change due to the higher fusion rate in the star. It will also put out enough hard radiation to kill anyone left here.

"I strongly suggest you start spinning up your drives and plot your jump back to Earth immediately, or you will risk being trapped and killed here.

"Weston out."

He cut the channel and, after an impossibly long heartbeat, fired the weapon.

"It's done," he said quietly. "Let's go."

THE BEACHES OUTSIDE WIRST'S SHOP on Clarion were as warm and sunny as they had been on Rake's previous visit, though now he had far more time and patience to enjoy them. And enjoying he was, sitting in the sand with a drink in his hand as he reflected on the wild course he had sailed since waking up in the insurance facility a month previous.

Three weeks had passed since they had fled the Last Redoubt, just minutes ahead of both the Terran fleet and Bruno's thugs. Fortunately, it had been time enough to begin their next sequence of jumps, and they had ultimately slipped pursuit by anyone angry enough to chase them down.

Rake had waited four days before sneaking back to Terra on a commercial flight under an assumed name. The insurance facility had refused to honor their quality-control policies due to Rake's time out in the Expanse, insisting that the damage to his nervous system could have been done by "user abuse" rather than any problem with their product.

Instead, he had been forced to use the insurance policy the Terran military had so conveniently purchased for him, ultimately finding himself in a new and healthy body - though leaving him without a safety net, as he couldn't afford another policy.

Both the Terran military and Oscar Bruno's operations had been quiet. A number of warships had been reported as lost, and the push by the Terran government to raise more money for military spending had been met with heavy public skepticism. Rake didn't doubt the short battle in the Last Redoubt had left the Terran military weaker than ever before; the odds of Terra successfully establishing a multi-system government through force, while poor after the devastation of the Great War, were now negligible.

Rake had tapped every contact he could still reach to find Oscar Bruno, but day-to-day operations of his criminal enterprises had all been turned over to his second, a sharp man named Ronan O'Dowd. Rumor had it that O'Dowd was Bruno's cousin, but Rake was far more concerned - and eventually relieved - by O'Dowd's lack of interest in finding the crew of the *Mirage*.

If he took over for Bruno, he's probably thanking me, Rake reflected. *Of course, I'm not going to go shake his hand and tell him what I did. I'll keep my head down, find some work, and not advertise what happened.*

Just as Bruno had told him, he had found Meg safe - after nearly a week of tracking. She had left Earth on a shuttle and found her way back to Clarion, where she was working with Wirst temporarily until she found someplace to settle in and set up a new pub.

The Lantash smuggler hole on the ring had been incommunicado since the Terran bombardment. Several Lantash patrol vessels had remained there in orbit after the Terrans' departure, and the fate of the occupants was still unknown.

Caree had vanished from the face of the Expanse. Without a ship to track her by, it would have been difficult to get any information, but every one of Rake's contacts came up completely empty-handed. Even the information he could get from inside Bruno's organization couldn't answer the simplest questions, like whether she had gone to the Last Redoubt. Every query hit a wall before finding an answer, forcing Rake to conclude that she was dead.

Even if I have to believe she's dead, she'll probably show up at the worst time possible and backblade me again. With insurance policies, it's always possible.

He wasn't sure how he felt about Caree's presumed death. He was angry with her, of course - she had played him masterfully, manipulated him at each step of the way to ensure he never suspected her, never thought for a moment she was working for anyone but herself.

But after his confrontation with Bruno on the supercruiser, he had begun to doubt her intentions. Certainly, she had wanted to turn over his information to the crime lord - but had she done so with the knowledge that Bruno intended to leave him alive?

The uncertainty gnawed at him a bit, and with each day he spent on the beaches of Clarion the anger he felt toward Caree faded.

The pilot was interrupted from his musings by a flash of blue hair as a woman sat down next to him on the beach. Rake glanced over at her, then gazed more openly and appreciatively when he realized how little she was wearing.

"Quit staring," the skiptracer said casually. "You'll get to see plenty of this, if you stick around."

"I don't have anywhere else to be," he said lightly.

"Not what I meant," Gail said, her voice teasing but with an undercurrent of seriousness. "Have you decided?"

"Decided what?"

"What you're going to do when you leave Clarion."

Rake glanced around theatrically before saying, "I don't see much reason to leave. Nice weather, sandy beaches, half-naked girl..."

"Woman," she corrected.

"Definitely woman," he grinned.

"You haven't answered my question."

He sighed and rubbed his eyes wearily. "Not yet, no," he admitted. "I'm sure I could find some smuggling jobs, or maybe even some piracy work, or *something*, but I'm not going to be in a hurry until I know that no one's trying to stick a knife in my back for what happened at the Last Redoubt."

"My proposal would help with that," she suggested gently. "You're pretty decent in a fight, and I need a ship."

"I'm no skiptracer," he said flatly. "It's too much like soldiering - don't ask questions, don't think beyond how to outmaneuver or outsmart your opponent, and take him down with maximum force. I'm done enough of that already."

She eyed him skeptically. "You can't imagine taking up a soldier's life again? Mercenary work would still suit you, if nothing else. But if you came with me, we could use the Network to keep an eye out for any jobs aimed at you."

He shook his head. "No, not going to happen."

They fell into a companionable silence for several long minutes, listening to nothing but the waves lap on the shore. Gail finally broke the silence by asking, "Ever since we left the Last Redoubt, you've been lost in thought, for weeks now. Is there something you need to tell me?"

Rake hesitated as he struggled to put it into words. When he did speak, it was slow and halting as he tried to keep his thoughts ordered. "Well, I told you the only thing I could imagine everyone was after - the only thing that was worth sending the entire Terran fleet after one person - was the Catalyst. And you agreed that it made sense, and we had to get rid of it."

Gail nodded agreeably. "Right with you so far."

"But when we boarded the supercruiser, it only had a few Terran ships harassing it. *And* Shoram was able to grab the Catalyst and load it on the ship without any real interference. *And* we walked right up to Bruno and he let us go again." Rake sighed and bowed his head to study the sand at his feet. "If they were all after the Catalyst, it wouldn't have been that easy. Bruno should have had thugs in the hangar, and the Terrans should have had most of their fleet concentrating on it."

"So you're afraid they were after something else," Gail said.

Rake whipped his head around to stare the blue-haired woman squarely in the eye. "You've been thinking about it, too."

She nodded in agreement. "It was too easy to get in, get the weapon, and get out. If that's really what everyone was after, they were pretty damned incompetent at the end there. And the way Bruno snared you with Caree and her crew, and the number of times the Terrans tracked you down when you were running from them - neither side would have screwed up that badly at the end."

"I was hoping I was imagining it," Rake admitted. "So the question, then, is what were they really after?"

"The Last Redoubt itself?" Gail asked dubiously. "There were shipyards and supplies in the system, weren't there?"

"I went back and looked through all the recorded sensor data, and there wasn't much left of the shipyards," he mused. "And there were a couple of planets nearby, but none of them were much more than rocks - the whole system is pretty young, astronomically speaking."

"Mining, then? Maybe the planets were great sources of raw materials."

"No, they were focusing on the ships," he contradicted. "Both Bruno and the Terrans were focusing all their efforts on the ships."

The answer struck him, and he turned to stare dumbfounded at the skiptracer, but her expression mirrored his own. "The ships," they said together.

Rake felt like slapping himself. "Of course - that's what they were after the whole time. Both the Earth and Terran navies from the Great War, all waiting for someone to stop by and patch them up and point them at an enemy."

"So now either Bruno or the Terrans have a whole new fleet," Gail said, her tone sinking into mournful tones. "We unleashed a big gun on the Expanse, and no one is ready for it."

"It's not as bad as it sounds," the ex-officer said, running through the logic. "No matter which side wound up with the Lost Fleets, it takes time to refurbish the ships and get them ready for real combat. The Terran military isn't exactly pulling in billions in taxes anymore, and even Bruno's full criminal empire would have trouble funding it. Not to mention the people they'd need to recruit and train to field those fleets - we're talking hundreds of thousands of personnel just for the ships, and by the time you add in the logistics, it'd be millions new uniforms."

"Does that make you feel any better about it?"

"Not really, no. You?"

"Not even a little."

Rake laid back on the sand, eyes closed, soaking in the warmth. "There's nothing we can do about it now," he said slowly. "And we kept the Catalyst out of everyone's hands - if we hadn't done that, someone would have wound up with a superweapon, and that would have been even worse."

He could sense Gail beside him, and couldn't help but peek through mostly-lidded eyes to admire her.

"It could be worse," she agreed. "With the logistics involved, it will be years before those ships see action. The Expanse can change an awful lot in that time."

Silence reigned for several more minutes as the two of them enjoyed the peaceful beach. It was Gail who broke the silence again. "Tomorrow, I'm going to catch an airskimmer into the starport and see what I can find for a ship and a ride off this rock. Unlike you, I have bills to pay and work to do."

"I have plenty of bills to pay," Rake said. "I've just been ignoring them. Sooner or later, though, I'll have to get back to work so I can start paying them off before you come hunting for me." He chuckled, a little humor to offset the gloom that had fallen over them. "I've got a pilot AI and a ship, so I should be okay."

"I'd hardly need to come hunting for you, Weston," Gail said, her voice sultry.

He opened his eyes, saw hers just centimeters from his own.

"I've already caught you."

A PERSONAL NOTE FROM THE AUTHOR

Thank you for buying *Dead Man's Fugue*. I hope you've enjoyed your journey with Rake Weston across the Expanse. The good news is that Rake's story isn't done yet! His tale continues with *Contract Hunt*, which will be released before Christmas.

Please take a minute to review *Dead Man's Fugue* on Amazon. Every new review helps my book's visibility on Amazon, which means I can commit more time to writing exciting new stories!

Lastly, if you'd like to know when I have new stories coming out, sign up for my mailing list or visit www.WritingUnderDuress.com so I can keep you up-to-date with the latest happenings.

Thanks again, and happy reading!

ABOUT THE AUTHOR

CASEY NEUMILLER is a full-time author who grew up in North Dakota. In 2008 he graduated from Dickinson State University with degrees in Computer Science and English. After five years working in Information Technology, he decided to start using his second degree.

He currently resides in North Dakota with his wife. In his non-writing time he hunts and fishes, enjoys online gaming, and plays amateur mechanic and carpenter.

Dead Man's Fugue is Neumiller's debut novel and the first in the Shattered Expanse series. His current writing projects include a sequel, *Contract Hunt*, and a new high fantasy series, beginning with *Destiny's Heir*.